D1330018

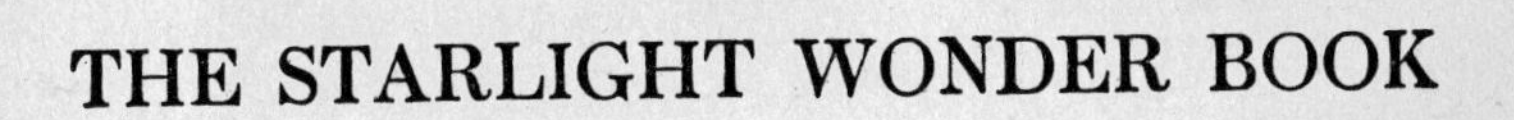

THE STARLIGHT WONDER BOOK

Long and hard fought Thyrza, and presently a great gust of the gale swept her against the Bell of the Sea

The STARLIGHT WONDER BOOK

By HENRY B. BESTON

AUTHOR OF
The FIRELIGHT FAIRY BOOK

WITH ILLUSTRATIONS BY
MAURICE DAY

The ATLANTIC MONTHLY PRESS
BOSTON

PRINTED IN THE UNITED STATES OF AMERICA

To
MISS MABEL DAVISON
MY WAR-TIME GODMOTHER
with the
HOMAGE
and
GRATEFUL AFFECTION
of
H·B·B·

CONTENTS

ILLUSTRATIONS

THE STARLIGHT WONDER BOOK

THE BRAVE GRENADIER

ONCE upon a time, during a great battle which was fought through the night in a tempest of lightning and rain, a brave young grenadier came upon one of the enemy lying sorely wounded on the field. Taking pity upon his foeman, the soldier bound up his wounds and carried him from the battle to the shelter of a little wood. Scarce had the wounded youth opened his eyes, when amid a blinding flash of lightning and a peal of tumbling thunder, a green chariot drawn by green dragons rushed downward through the hurrying clouds and sank to earth at the soldier's side. Bidding the dragons be still, a tall, dark, and stately man wearing a long green mantle descended from the chariot, took the wounded lad in his arms, and thus addressed the grenadier: —

"Generous friend, to you I owe the life of my youngest son. I am the Enchanter of the Green

Glen. Take you this little green wand in memory of the great debt I owe you. Whatsoever you strike once with it will continue to grow larger till you cry 'stop'; whatsoever you strike twice with it will grow smaller till you bid the magic cease. Farewell, brave soldier, and may good fortune walk forever by your side."

Then, wrapping his wide green mantle about the body of his son, the Wizard bade his scaly, yellow-eyed dragons be on their way, and vanished on high in the tempest and the dark.

And now the wars were over and done, and the soldier found himself mustered out and turned loose to earn his living in the world. Still clad in his grenadier's uniform, and wearing his blue greatcoat buttoned close about him, he slung his knapsack to his shoulder, fastened it to his belt in front by crossed straps of white leather, put on his big shiny hat, and turned from the camp over the hills and far away.

It was the early autumn of the year: great

roaring gusts swept by overhead, singing shrilly through the withered leaves still clinging to the branches, apples lay red ripe in the frost-nipped grass, and the country folk were gleaning in the stubble of the fields. On through the villages went the soldier, hoping to find work for the winter among the farms; he knocked at this door and at that, but ever in vain. Presently the mighty summits of the Adamant Mountains, gleaming with new-fallen snow, rose beyond the bare woods and the lonely fields. Following the great royal road, the soldier tramped on into the very heart of the mountain mass.

"Perhaps I shall meet with better luck in the kingdoms beyond the peaks," thought the grenadier, as he trudged along. How still it was! Now the soldier could hear the roaring of the river in the gorge below the road, now the cry of the eagles circling high above some desolate crag.

At high noon on the third day, the soldier

arrived at the brazen column which marks the descent of the royal road to the kingdoms beyond the hills. A biting wind, keen with the smell of snow, blew from the surrounding peaks, and made the soldier very hungry indeed. Sheltering himself against the giant column, he slipped his knapsack from his shoulder, and looked within for the last of the bread and cheese which a good wife of the mountain villages had given him the day before. Alas, there was but the tiniest crust of bread to be found, and the littlest crumb of cheese! Suddenly, as he fished about in the sack, the grenadier discovered the little green wand. He had quite forgotten it. A notion came into his head to try the magic, and he struck the bit of bread *one* smart tap.

The moment he did so, the fragment of bread bounced a few inches into the air, and fell back to the ground; soon it was the size of a loaf of bread; a moment or two later the loaf had grown to the size of a table; soon the mass of bread was the size of a small house. And it was growing, growing, growing.

"Stop!" cried the soldier. The magic ceased. The soldier struck the mountain of bread *twice.*

Again it leaped into the air, but this time it began to grow less. Like to a candle end in the fire, it began to vanish before the soldier's eyes. Presently it was once more the size of a generous loaf, and thus the soldier bade it remain. Next he enchanted the bit of cheese to an ample size, and found himself provided with victuals fit for a king. Later, when he had eaten his fill, he amused himself by enchanting a pebble into a great rock. And that rock may be seen in the Adamant Mountains *to this very day!*

At the end of a week's journey the soldier reached the Golden Plain, which lies between the Adamant Mountains and the sea.

Now at the time of the soldier's arrival, the people of the Golden Plain were being day by day swept to hunger and ruin by the devastation wrought throughout their land by a hippodrac. Driven by hunger, so some thought, from its stony lair in the forests of the sun, this terrible creature had suddenly swooped down on the harvest fields a month before, and had roamed the land till the precious grain had for the most part been consumed or destroyed. Worse yet, the hippodrac was even then breaking open the royal granaries, in which lay such grain as the citizens had been able to store away.

This terrible creature, I must tell you, was a kind of fearsome winged horse. It was larger than any earthly animal, black as midnight in color, and armored over the chest and head with a sheath of dragon's scales. Add to this a pair of giant wings, black and lustrous as a raven's, a wicked horse-like head with huge jaws, hoofs of blue steel, and an appetite like a devouring flame, and you will see that the people of the Golden Plain had true cause for alarm. Black wings outspread, blue hoofs plunging, roaring from the fiery pits of its violet nostrils, the hippodrac was master in the land.

In the hope of ridding themselves of the monster, the people of the Golden Plain offered a huge treasure to whosoever might conquer the invader. In true soldier fashion the grenadier resolved to fight the hippodrac, and win fame and fortune at a blow.

Now the Lord Chancellor of the realm, who ruled the land during the minority of the Princess Mirabel, had no intention whatever of paying the promised reward. Not only had this wicked man stolen so much money from the royal treasury that scarce was a penny left, but also was he miserly, cruel, and avaricious. Torn between fear of the hippodrac and fear of having to empty his own money-bags of the stolen gold in order to pay the reward, the Chancellor wandered back and forth all day through the castle halls. Thus far, however, no one had ever returned to claim the treasure.

After talking with some who had seen the

hippodrac, the soldier retired to a little inn to make his plans. Sitting alone in a great settle by the fire, he watched the flames grow ruddier as the afternoon sun sank below the western hills. Presently it was night, a night quiet, cool, and bright with great winter stars.

The grenadier made his way unobserved out of the royal city, and soon arrived in the midst of the ruined and trampled fields. Here the grain had been gathered, bound in sheaves, and left to perish when the harvesters fled; here the uncut stalks had withered in the ground; here stood a house from which everyone had run for his life. Presently the soldier beheld, standing apart on a lonely hill, the crumbling towers of the ruined castle which served as the hippodrac's den.

A late, wasted, half-moon began to rise. The soldier made his way up the slope, and peered through the doorless portal into the moonlit ruin.

At the end of the great entrance-hall of the

castle, its monstrous head resting on the lowest step of the winding stair which led to the roofless banqueting-hall above, lay the monster. The rays of the waning moon, slanting through the broken tracery of a great window, fell on its vast bulk; a rumbling breathing alone disturbed the starry silence of the night.

"I must make my way down those stairs," said the grenadier to himself, and crept off to seek a way to the banqueting hall above. Finally he managed to find a little stairway in a ruined turret. Creeping along softly, ever so softly, over the floor of the banqueting hall, he reached the head of the great stair and looked down its curving steps to the monster asleep below. Then, step by step by step, the grenadier approached the hippodrac.

Suddenly the soldier's foot dislodged a piece of clattering stone. The hippodrac awoke with a scream, but the soldier struck it *two* swift taps with the little green wand.

The instant he did so, the hippodrac uttered

a cry of fright and rage which waked the good folk of the city in their beds, and bounced, wings beating wildly, in the air. The grenadier took refuge at the head of the balustrade. Smaller and smaller grew the furious and bewildered beast. Now it had shrunk to the size of a pony, now it had dwindled to the size of a dog, now it was scarce larger than a kitten.

"Stop!" cried the grenadier. Wild with fright, the tiny monster took wing, and fluttered like a terrified bird into a corner of the ruins. And there, beating about and flapping its wings madly, the grenadier caught it in his high hat, and shook it into his knapsack. This done, he walked swiftly back to the inn, and went to bed.

Now one of the Lord Chancellor's rascals had been on watch for his return, and when the grenadier returned with the light of victory in his eyes, this spy ran to inform his rogue of a master. Suspecting magic of some kind, the wicked Chancellor made his way to the inn, and stole the green wand while the soldier slept.

Suddenly the soldier's foot dislodged a piece of clattering stone, and the hippodrac awoke

Early the next morning, the soldier sent word to the counselors of court that he had mastered the hippodrac, and waited their good pleasure to prove the truth of his word. Within a very short time a royal messenger appeared, summoning him before the assembled court at the tenth hour.

And now the soldier, carrying the tiny hippodrac in his knapsack, was led to the judgment hall of the royal palace. The Princess Mirabel sat on the throne of the realm, whilst the Lord Chancellor stood by her side, a smile of triumph on his wicked lips. But the soldier had eyes only for the young Princess, who was as fair as the first wild rose of the year. As for the Princess, it must be confessed that she thought the stalwart young grenadier with the black hair and the blue eyes quite the most pleasant person she had ever seen.

Simply and modestly the grenadier told the story of his capture of the hippodrac. Leaning forward a little, the Princess listened eagerly.

"And your proof of this — ?" questioned the Lord Chancellor.

"Is here," replied the grenadier, and opening his knapsack, he took from it the hippodrac and placed it on the carpet just before the throne. As the soldier had taken the precaution to clip the monster's wings, the tiny thing could do naught but dance with rage on its little blue hoofs, and lash out madly right and left in a frenzy of fear. A murmur of astonishment rose from the assembly. There was a great craning of necks. All present looked at the Lord Chancellor to hear what he might say.

"That little thing, the great hippodrac?" said the Lord Chancellor, evilly. "Pooh! 'T is a juggler's kitten, rather. I shall give no reward for this."

"You dare?" cried the grenadier fiercely. "Wait!" And he reached in his pocket for the little green wand, but, alas, the little green wand was gone.

"Pooh!" said the Chancellor again, watching,

with contented eyes, the poor grenadier madly thrusting his hands into every pocket, "You see he cannot do as he pretends. The fellow is an impostor. Ho, guards! Take this rogue and his dancing kitten off to prison."

"But it looks like the hippodrac," protested the Princess.

"No! Not a bit of it, not a bit of it!" roared the Chancellor. And he quickly silenced all those who were fain to see justice done, by threatening to send any objector to the royal diamond-mines in the Adamant Mountains.

Left to himself in a lonely cell of the royal prison, the poor grenadier awaited the day of his departure for the mines. Finding the time hang heavy on his hands, he amused himself by trying to tame the tiny hippodrac. To his surprise and pleasure, the fierce little creature made a swift response. Soon it was eating crumbs from his hand. In a fortnight it could spell out words and letters by tapping the floor with its right foreleg! And day by day, its clipped wings grew once more to full size. "Oh, if you could only get me my green wand again!" said the soldier one morning.

At these words, the hippodrac beat an excited tattoo on the table, and before the soldier could seize it, spread its little gleaming wings, and fled through the barred window out into the world.

All day long the soldier waited its return. "It has flown away forever," he thought, as twilight fell. A moment later, however, he heard a whir of tiny wings, and the hippodrac returned, the little green wand in its jaws. You may well believe that the soldier was overjoyed! That very night he found means to send a petition to the Princess, asking to be brought before her that he might at last prove the truth of his story.

Now the Chancellor, knowing that his wicked scheme had succeeded, and never dreaming of the possibility of the grenadier's escape, had gone a-hunting; so the Princess took matters into her own hands, and next morning summoned the grenadier before the court. Alas! Just as the grenadier reached the throne, the Chancellor, hastily summoned by another of his rascally spies, came striding angrily into the judgment hall.

"What means this?" he roared. "How came that fellow to be out of prison? Ho, guards, take him back at once!"

"No!" said the little Princess bravely. "I believe in him, and he shall have justice in my realm!"

"Do you dare defy me?" cried the Chancellor. "Guards, do your duty! I am Regent here."

A handful of soldiers strode toward the grenadier. With a smile on his lips and in his eyes, the grenadier struck the hippodrac *one* smart tap with the magic wand.

The creature bounced, and instantly began to increase in size; suddenly it snorted fiercely and reared on its hind legs; once again it screamed even such a scream as it had uttered when the grenadier enchanted it in the ruined castle. People began to fly pell-mell in every direction. Only Mirabel, who was a lass of spirit, stood her ground.

When the hippodrac had reached its full size, the soldier cried "Stop!" Then, for a moment, the monster and the man gazed directly into each other's eyes. The soldier still smiled.

The hippodrac had understood.

Uttering now the angriest cry of all, the creature darted forward, and seized the Lord Chancellor by the scruff of his ugly neck. Then opening wide its giant wings, it leaped up on all four legs, and flying down the vast hall, crashed through a great window and out into the freedom of the cloudless sky. So terrified was it by its experiences, that it flew back to its lair in the forests of the sun, and never bothered anybody any more.

On the way home, while flying at a great height, it got bored with carrying the Lord Chancellor and let him drop. No one has since heard of this personage. No one ever will.

When the excitement subsided, the citizens hailed the grenadier as the preserver of their country and offered him the treasure which the Chancellor had stolen away. But the grenadier had already found a treasure much more to his liking — the Princess Mirabel. The handsome young couple were married with great pomp and ceremony on New Year's day.

And thus the brave grenadier became a king, and with Mirabel by his side, ruled over the Golden Plain for many a long and happy year.

THE PALACE OF THE NIGHT

Once upon a time there was an Emperor of the Isles, who had but one son, the Prince Porphyrio. On the day which beheld the Prince's coming of age, the Emperor summoned the youth to his council chamber, and said to him: —

"Dear son, when you were a little child, I pledged to you the hand of the Lady Liria, daughter of my friend and ally, the Emperor of the Plain. You are now of age, and I would fain send you forth to find the Princess and win her for your own."

Then replied the tall, golden-haired Prince, "Dear father, give me but a brave ship and a gallant crew, and I will this very eve set sail for the Emperor's city and greet the Lady Liria."

Pleased with this speech, the Emperor gave orders that a fine ship be swiftly prepared for the voyage. And this was done.

And now it was night, and the vessel lay waiting, her sails gleaming green-white in the moonlight, her ladder shrouds gently swaying against the pale and starry sky. When came the ebb of the midnight tide, the anchors were weighed, the great sails trimmed to the breeze, and the vessel piloted forth to the measureless plain of the sea.

Now it came to pass, as the great ship sped upon her furrowed way, that Porphyrio took it into his head to visit the Fair of the Golden Bear, and fled before the wind to the festival city. Little by little — for the air was but light — the ship left behind her the blue of the deeps, and entered the green waters of the shallows. Suddenly there was a cry of "Land Ho!" and from afar, over the landward hastening waves, Porphyrio beheld the great tower of the Fair. A giant golden image of a bear, standing erect, crowned the high tower-top, and shone dully bright above the haze.

At sundown the Prince, accompanied by his mariners, found himself in the midst of the great Fair, in the very heart of the din, the medley of outlandish costumes, the babel of strange tongues, and the shrill cries of the shopmen and the merchants. Surely there was never such a market place as the Fair of the Golden Bear!

Everything in the world was there to be bought and sold. At one booth a venerable man in a scholar's gown and velvet cap sold words — rare words, rich words, strange words, beautiful words, and drove a brisk trade with a crowd of poets and lovers; at another an old woman in green sold rosy glasses to those who were at outs with the world; and at still another a joyous fellow in blue offered sunbeams, which he had caught in a mirror and imprisoned in bits of magic glass.

Porphyrio was quite delighted with the sunbeams, which shone night and day, like diamonds aflame with golden fires. "The Lady Liria will surely be pleased with one of these," thought he, and purchased the finest of all.

Now it came to pass that, as he walked about the Fair with his retinue of sailor-men, Porphyrio caught sight of a rustic fellow in brown corduroys who was carrying a sea bird in a wicker cage. And because he loved the wild folk of the sea, the Prince said to the countryman: —

"Good friend, whither go you with your bird?"

"To the animal merchants, sir," replied the fellow. "'Tis a wild bird which I found in my field on a morning after a storm. Only look, sir; it wears a circle of feathers on its head, for all the world like a crown."

"Why, so it does!" said the young Prince. "Come, will you sell him to me?"

"Oh yes, indeed, sir," replied the countryman. "'Tis yours for a florin of gold and a penny of silver." And he held out his hand for the sum.

"Good!" said Porphyrio, and he paid the money. Then, to the countryman's amazement, he threw open the door of the cage, and allowed the sea bird to escape. With a glad cry, and a mighty beating of its gray wings, the creature climbed into a splendor of the sunset, dwindled to a black speck, and vanished from their eyes.

Once more the Prince set sail. For a few days the weather remained tranquil and fair. Then came a night of cloud, and a rushing wind, which increased during the day to a hurricane. Now arose a great din, the howling of the wind through the shrouds, the cracking and straining of the timbers of the ship, the cries of the sailors, and the roaring and foaming of the deep. All night long, through the wild ocean dark, the Prince's ship drifted nearer and nearer the unknown waters of the Southern Sea. Suddenly, just before the dawn, a tremendous noise was heard; the vessel trembled throughout her length, and crashing down once more on a hidden reef, broke apart. A huge wave swept Porphyrio from the deck, some wreckage hurled itself upon him, and he knew no more.

When he woke again, close upon noon, he found that the waves had carried him to the stony beach of a dark and unknown isle. A stately wall of cliffs of the strangest dark-blue stone girdled it about; to the left, to the right, the rampart swept, solemn, unscalable, and huge. One broken mast of the Prince's ship still rose forlorn above the tumbling waters on the reefs; but of the gallant crew there was never a sign. With a heavy heart Porphyrio trudged off to look for shelter and for aid. Long hours followed he the curving shore, even till the sun, which had been shining in his face, little by little crept to the side and shone behind, yet never a way to the headland's height stood forth in the sheer and sombre wall.

And now, of a sudden, and by great good fortune, — for the tide was rising, — Porphyrio, turning the base of an advancing crag, found himself close by a noble promontory that sloped from the cliff-top to foundations in the sea. Half climbing, half dragging himself along the stones and terraces of this ridge, the Prince attained at last the height of the blue wall.

A great dark isle lay open before him — a solitary isle of shadowy lands, gloomy woods, and rocks and hillocks of the same dark stone he had marked before. Save for the faint murmur of the encircling sea below and the sighing of the wind, the isle was as silent as a land beneath the deep: indeed, so still and dark it was, that it seemed as if the night reigned there, forever untroubled by the day. In the very heart of the gloom, its mighty walls and blue battlements lifted high against cloud mountains gathered in the west, a stately palace rose.

After a long, winding journey through a wood dark as a leafy cave, Porphyrio arrived at the portals of the dwelling.

The palace was as silent as a stone. Of silver were its massy doors, and they were sealed and barred, and from turret to foundation stone its windows were with silver shutters closed against the day. Not a sign or a memory of living things was there to be seen.

Wondering in his heart at the mystery, Porphyrio presently made his way into a noble garden, wherein were pools and basins of blue water rimmed about with silver, and tall, dark trees stately as night. Again to his wonderment, the Prince beheld that the flowers in the garden were such as opened only in the night — the pale, fragrant jasmine hid there, the moonflower dreamed, and the shy star-daisy gathered her petals before her face.

Suddenly the Prince heard steps behind him, and turning swiftly, beheld a fair Princess gazing at him with eyes in which wonder, alarm, and hope might all be seen.

"Speak! Who are you? What do you here?" said the Princess quickly.

To this Porphyrio replied that he was a prince who had been shipwrecked on a voyage. And he told the Princess of his adventures.

"Alas," replied the lady, "You have come to the dark land! Know you not into whose power you have fallen? This dark isle is the dwelling of the Magician of the Night, who rules the fairy world from sunset to the morn. When comes the dawn, his mighty power wanes, and he and his people of the night hasten to this locked and shuttered palace, here to lie hidden from the sunlight which is their enemy and deadly fear. I alone go forth, for I, alas, am a mortal. But hearken to my story.

"I am the Princess Liria (Porphyrio started). My father is the Emperor of the Plain. On midsummer eve, as I was walking with my handmaidens in the garden, a messenger from my father arrived bidding me come at once to the great hall of state. I obeyed the message, and going to the hall, found there the Magician of the Night, who had just presented a haughty petition for my hand. Because of his fear of the Magician, my father was very ill at ease. All looked to me for an answer. I replied courteously that, though I felt highly honored at the demand, I nevertheless felt bound to refuse, for I had been affianced since childhood to another. For you must know, good Prince, that my father was long the true friend and ally of the Emperor of the Isles, and had pledged my hand to his only son, the Prince Porphyrio.

"Would that this were all I had to tell! But — woe to me! — scarce had the Magician, with a mocking smile, bowed low and disappeared into the night, when a terrible storm of his contriving descended upon our unfortunate city, overturning our tallest towers and strewing ruin far and wide. Our torches quenched by the rain and wind, my maidens and I took refuge in a great chamber of the north turret. At the height of the storm the wind suddenly burst open the double portals, there came a great flash of lightning and a roar of thunder, and I beheld the Magician standing tall and motionless between the doors, surrounded by a dozen of his creatures of the night. I cried out, but his servants seized me and led me forth; great wings bore me upward through the very torment of the heavens, a darkness fell on me, and I knew no more. When I awoke, I found myself here in the Palace of the Night.

"Farewell, dear land of the Golden Plain, whose harvests I shall never more see! Farewell, dear Prince Porphyrio of the Isles!"

"But I am Porphyrio!" cried the Prince, "and I was on my way to find you, noble Liria, when the storm swept me to this isle."

You may be sure the heart of the Princess leaped when she heard these tidings!

Forgetting that he was himself but a shipwrecked wanderer much in need of aid, the Prince, like the brave fellow that he was, could think of nothing but of rescuing his lady from the dark magician; as for the Princess, she could think of naught but the plight of Porphyrio, tossed friendless and forlorn upon the isle. But at length she shook her head and smiled.

"To-day," said she, "is mine, and to-morrow also; but the Magician has bidden me be prepared for the wedding feast by sundown on the following day. But, look, the shield of the sun breaks the storm clouds close above the waters; twilight approaches; the hour of the magician is at hand; you must go. Hide yourself well to-night, and come to the garden to-morrow when the chimes ring thrice. On yon dark wall you will find some strangely shaped fruits growing; fear not to eat of them when you hunger. Liria the Unhappy bids you farewell, Prince Porphyrio."

"Farewell, Princess," replied Porphyrio. "Do not despair. We shall yet outwit the dark Magician!"

And now the Prince lay hid in the heart of a great tree, watching the doors and windows of the palace slowly opening in the twilight. Suddenly huge bells swung forth in waves of heavy sound, strange music played, and the thousand windows filled with the magic glow of moon-fire. All night long the people of the night held festival; but at the break of dawn the silver windows closed slowly on their hinges, the music grew faint, and the murmur died away.

On the second afternoon the Prince, in his impatience, came early to the shadowy garden. The Princess Liria was not to be found, so Porphyrio wandered away into the dark alleys by the pools. Suddenly he found himself looking at his own reflection in a huge round mirror which two marble statues supported between them, one at each side. Happening to move a little, the Prince discovered that his reflection did not move! He lifted an arm, the image remained motionless; he shook his head, the mirror gave no sign. Puzzled, Porphyrio left the spot, and saw his reflection remaining behind the glass.

Presently he heard the welcome footsteps of Liria. And as the lovers walked and talked and discussed plans of escape, the Prince chanced to tell of the mirror he had found. Uttering a little gasp of alarm, the Princess cried: "Now we are lost indeed! Yon mirror is a mirror of memory, and reveals to the Magician the faces of those who walk these paths. As soon as he sees your reflection therein, — and he gazes into the glass every eve,— his demons will be sent in search of you. There is one hope and one only.

"Go you once more to the sea; follow the cliff for a league to the west of the promontory, and you will find at its base the opening of an ocean cave. When you arrive there the tide will be at half-flood, and the entrance will still be visible above the waves. Fight your way within and climb to the cavern's height. Little by little the rising tide will seal the portal and hide you from the search. Make haste, dear Porphyrio, for there is not an instant to lose! Oh, that I had warned you!"

Ragingly angry with himself for being a meddlesome fool, Porphyrio hurried down to the sea and sought out the cave. Twilight was at hand; the tide was rising fast, already the

The image in the mirror stood still

entrance was almost closed by the sea. Buffeted by the breakers and tossed against the cliff as he strode, the Prince at length made his way into the cave and climbed to a shelf of rock above the height of the tide. A few minutes later, the water closed the entrance completely, thus imprisoning Porphyrio in a hollow darkness through which the ebb and flow of the outer sea swept with chuckles and whispering laughter. All night long waited Porphyrio in the cold, watery dark.

Toward the end of the Prince's vigil, the earth suddenly shook, the waters hushed, and through the silence and the dark Porphyrio heard the long thunder of a mighty overthrow.

"What can that be?" thought he.

When the first red rays of the sun streamed along the rocky floor of the cave, Porphyrio descended from his refuge, and walked out of the cave-mouth to the sea.

Now, as Porphyrio walked along the shore, it came to pass that he discerned, deeply embedded in the bluish sands and lashed about with ropes of matted weed, the splendid painted chest which had lain in his cabin on the ship. Its brazen lock, though tarnished by the waters, was still highly clasped; but sea and stone had broken the wood loose from the hasps, and the Prince had little difficulty in raising the lid. With a rueful smile he gazed down into his robes and fine array lying musty and sand-strewn within. There lay his prince's circlet of gold, here his jeweled sword of state, here the rich gifts he had meant for the Princess Liria. And among these, tucked away in the very corner of the chest, Porphyrio found the sunbeam he had purchased at the Fair of the Golden Bear.

"Were Liria armed with this," cried he, "the Magician of the Night could not prevail against her!" At the thought, a new strength leaped in his weary heart, and he hurried along the cliff toward the promontory. The storm had now cleared away, the ocean thundered and broke into silvery white foam at the foot of the blue ramparts, and the Isle of the Night raised itself defiantly against a bright and royal sun.

The Magician, however, had not been idle. The mirror had told its story; a search had been made; a legion of creatures had sought Porphyrio in every corner of the isle. Compelled by the approach of dawn to abandon this pursuit, the Magician resolved to render the island unapproachable from the sea. With a spell of tremendous power he caused the promontory to break from the other cliff and fall in scattered and monstrous ruin to the beach below. It was the thunder of this overthrow which had shaken the earth and sounded through the cave.

As a last precaution, the Magician forbade Liria to leave the Palace of the Night, and locked and sealed the doors and windows, every one.

Presently the Prince, hastening along the beach, came in sight of the ruined headland,

and a great fear laid its icy hand on his heart as he beheld the triumph of his enemy. How was he to reach the headland height? The cliff-wall now circled the entire island without a break. League after league he trudged, along the shore, through the tide, searching, searching for some way to scale the overhanging walls. Higher and higher climbed the sun. The shadows fell to the east, the afternoon waned, and still Porphyrio had found no path to the top. Desperate at last, he attempted to scale the steep face of the blue precipice. From ledge to ledge, climbing with torn fingers and aching arms, struggled the Prince, and presently, his further advance barred, fell backward, faint and overcome, on a shelf of rock high above the sea.

When his strength returned, he found himself close by an eyrie of sea birds brooding on their nests in shelves and rifts of the rock. With a great clamor of piping and crying the creatures rose startled from their nests, so filling the air with wings that Porphyrio closed his eyes. Suddenly the master of the eyrie, uttering a joyous call, swept down close to the Prince, and with an upward surge of his heart Porphyrio recognized the winged king whose freedom he had purchased at the Fair of the Golden Bear! And now the sea birds gathered about the Prince, some gathering folds of his garments into their talons, others lifting him on broad wings, till presently he was borne from the narrow ledge and the sound of the sea into the splendor and silence of the sky.

The end of day was at hand. Unveiled of any wisp of cloud, the fiery sun lay just above the western waters, its lower rim almost resting on the waves. Once again approached the hour of the Magician of the Night.

The cloud of sea birds flew inland over the blue isle, and settled to earth at the very doors of the Palace of the Night. And opening his arms to them, Porphyrio cried aloud his thanks as they wheeled and fled.

The Prince walked boldly to the great door, and blew a loud blast on the warder's horn. There came no answer to his call. The Palace of the Night remained silent and dark. The sun's rim dipped; a little breeze made its way from the sea through the mysterious gardens; the flowers of the night stirred like sleepers in a dream.

"O jewel of the sun," cried Porphyrio, "Give me now your aid!" And with these words he touched the sunbeam to the lock. A crack resounded, then a shattering crash, and the doors swung open wide. Hastening on twixt other and other doors and through heavy tapestries, Porphyrio at length found himself at the threshhold of the great hall of the Palace of the Night. Rich hangings of dark blue velvet, strewn with stars of silver and gold, hung from the giant walls; a thousand lamps of pale moon-fire swayed on silver chains from the unseen height o'erhead; there were huge columns, and dark aisles. To one side of the hall, by a silver throne raised upon a dais, stood the Magician of the Night, his arms folded on his breast. Proud and pale by his side, near a second throne, stood the Princess Liria. About them were gathered the people of the Night.

As the doors parted, all turned to gaze at Porphyrio.

Fixing his dark eyes upon the Prince, the Magician spake a terrible incantation; but his words shattered themselves against the sunbeam as a threatening wave breaks to drift and foam against a crag.

"Seize him!" commanded the Magician.

At these words a host of dark beings surged about Porphyrio, encircling him, yet afraid to attack. Porphyrio took Liria by the hand, and led her toward the door. But even as he did so, the Magician caused awesome silvery fires to bar the outward way.

At the horizon's edge, the waters were leaping up about the sun.

Baffled by the flame, Porphyrio, still guarding

Liria, fought his way toward a great stair at the very end of the hall. In the wall there, barred with silver and shuttered with stone, a giant circular window faced the west. And now there rose a tumult through the hall, and sounds of magic and thunder. Nothing daunted, Porphyrio touched the sunbeam to the window-bar, and threw the double shutters open wide. The sun was yet above the wave, sky and water were aflame, and the great tide of sunlight swept into the Palace of the Night like the music of many trumpets.

From all within the Palace a great wailing cry arose that presently died away. When Porphyrio and Liria turned to gaze, the Magician and his people had vanished, conquered and forever powerless. And the velvet hangings were but cobwebs clinging to the walls, and the lamps of moon-fire but empty shells.

Then Porphyrio and Liria walked hand in hand to the darkening sea, and beheld there a brave merchant-ship which the sea bird was guiding to the isle. You may be sure it did not take the jolly mariners long to rescue the lovers from the headland! And thus the Prince and Princess fared to Liria's realm, where there their marriage was celebrated with the greatest ceremony.

In time Porphyrio became a king and Liria a queen, and thus they lived happily ever after.

THE ENCHANTED BABY

ONCE upon a time the King of a great country had a quarrel with a goblin. Now it chanced that the King had the best of the dispute, and this so angered the goblin that he departed from the realm and cast about for an opportunity to do a mischief to his foe.

Now, as the goblin bided his time, it came to pass that the King and the Queen, who had long been childless, became the proud parents of a bouncing baby boy. From rosy summer morn to the murmuring quiet of a summer night, the whole realm gave itself over to rejoicing. Bells rang from the towers in cities and steeples in the fields, cannon boomed from castle towers, and small cakes, each one iced with the Prince's monogram in red and white sugar, were distributed by royal command among the children of the realm.

Now it was the custom of the country that

the heir to the throne be shown to the assembled nobility of the realm on the first day of his seventh week in this changing world of ours, and presently this day stood at hand upon the calendar.

On the afternoon of the ceremony, the scene within the great hall of the palace was magnificence itself! Assembled by thousands and ten thousands, the magnificoes of the land, all in ceremonial attire, moved or tried to move about; but as the huge hall was crowded to its bulging doors, this was difficult, and there were, I regret to say, the usual faintings from lack of air, cries of protest, bad-tempered pushing, caps knocked awry, crumpled ruffs, and lost jewels.

Suddenly the great bell of the palace set up a ponderous and solemn booming — the ceremony was about to begin! Mercilessly crowding back the already densely jammed magnificoes on the toes of still other magnificoes, a number of gentleman ushers contrived to open an aisle the length of the hall, and when this feat had been accomplished, the two tallest sergeants in the royal army opened the double portals leading forth from the royal drawing-room. And now, heralded by a great ringing peal of golden trumpets, and accompanied by a crash of exultant thunder on the palace organ, a noble procession slowly advanced through the gateway into the hall. The generalissimo of the royal armies came first, marching solemnly and quite alone, for he was marshal of the occasion; then came trumpeters in green and yellow; then a chosen detail of giant grenadiers dressed in rose-red and silver-grey; then pages scattering flowers from golden baskets; then a little space; and then, advancing with the dignity of a cloud, appeared the Lord Chancellor, wheeling in the baby.

Of finest yellow gold were the wheels and push-bar of the perambulator, whilst the carriage part had been hollowed from a single stupendous opal! Amid a deafening din of huzzas and shouts and bell clangs, the procession solemnly advanced to a dais raised at the head of the hall.

Suddenly an invisible shape fluttered in through a window, muttered something beside the baby's cradle, uttered a mocking goblin laugh, and fled away unperceived and unsuspected.

After wheeling the baby to the centre of the dais, the Lord Chancellor gave a signal to the trumpeters to break into the national anthem, and bent over the cradle to take the infant and show him to the throng. To his horror, the cradle was *empty!* The little Prince's pillow was there, the coverlet edged with turquoise, and the rattle filled with seed pearls — but no baby.

"The baby! The baby! Where 's the baby?" gulped the Lord Chancellor, scarce able to speak. An awkward pause followed: excited whispers, conjectures, rumors buzzed through the audience. Presently, as the truth began to spread, a growing uproar rocked the hall. Soon everybody was busily looking here and there — lifting up edges of carpets, poking about behind curtains, staring at the ceiling, and examining corners.

All at once a baby's cry was heard, faint to be sure, but quite unmistakable.

"Search, search, my friends!" cried the King. "The Grand Cross of the Order of the Bluebird to whosoever discovers my child!"

The baby's cry was heard again! Where could he be?

Suddenly a clever young lady-in-waiting, who had been searching the opal carriage, uttered a piercing shriek. While groping about in the perambulator, she had felt the baby, but had been unable to see him. Like a sudden crumbling of walls, the dreadful truth broke upon everyone present.

The baby had become invisible!

Invisible he was, and invisible he remained. You may well believe that his upbringing was indeed a difficult task! To make matters worse, it was soon discovered that not only was the Prince himself totally invisible, but also that such clothes as touched him became invisible, too. One could *feel* the little Prince, one could *hear* him — and that was all. Thus, if he crept away on the nursery floor, one had either to grope for him through the clear air, carefully feeling here and feeling there, or wait until he cried. No wonder the poor Queen was forever searching the land for new nurses-in-waiting, and forever sending home nurses whose nerves had proved unequal to the strain! One could never tell what might be happening.

On one occasion, for instance, the child actually managed to escape from his nursery to the sweeping lawns of the royal palace, and the entire national army, working in scout formation, had to spend the whole afternoon creeping about on its hands and knees before the prince was found asleep in the shelter of a plum tree.

Now, when every attempt to undo the spell

had failed, it came to pass that the King went to visit the Wise Man of Pansophia, a learned sage who sat in a wing chair beneath a green striped umbrella at the crossroads of the world, giving counsel to all comers. This sage was clad in the stately folds of a full black gown, a round black velvet cap rested on the crown of his snow-white head, a broad white beard lay spread upon his breast, and on his nose were huge round spectacles, over whose edge he looked with an air of solemn authority.

Beginning at the umbrella, an army of questioners, patiently waiting in single file, stretched dozens of miles across the rolling land and disappeared, still unbroken, over the crest of a distant hill. These patient folk, it is a pleasure to relate, courteously gave way to the unhappy King.

When he had heard the King's story, the Wise Man shook his venerable head, and replied in a voice which sounded like the booming of waves on a resounding shore: —

"The spell which binds your son is a mighty one, and can only be removed by touching him with the spell-dispeller, the all-powerful talisman given your ancestor, King Decimo, by his fairy bride."

"Alas," replied the King, "the spell-dispeller was stolen from the royal treasury twenty years ago. Could you not tell us who stole it, or where it may be found?"

"Was it not the only spell-dispeller in the whole wide world?" questioned the Wise Man.

"It was," replied the King with a sad, assenting nod.

"Then it was stolen from you by the Master Thief of the Adamant Mountains," boomed the Wise Man.

"And perhaps *you* can tell us where *he* can be found," said the King. The Wise Man shook his head.

"Ask me where lies the raindrop which fell yesterday in the river," replied the Wise Man, "but ask me not where dwells the Master

Thief. I do not know. No one knows. But as for breaking the spell, it is the spell-dispeller or nothing. Would that I could help you more!"

And, bidding the King a ceremonious farewell, the sage turned his attention to the questioner at the head of the long line, a stout peasant-fellow whose cottage chimney failed to draw.

But now you must hear of the Master Thief of the Adamant Mountains.

This mysterious personage, of whom all had heard, but whom none had seen, dwelt in a secret house in a lost valley of the mountains, a house so artfully shaped and so cunningly concealed with vines and branches, that the very birds of the air were deceived by it and would often come to roost on the chimney, mistaking it for a chestnut tree! As for the Master Thief himself, a kind of living bean-pole was he, for he was taller than the tallest, leaner than the leanest, and provided with a pair of long, tireless legs which could outrun and outlast the swiftest coursers in the land.

During the night, he moved through the world in a strange garment of pitchy blue-black, fitted as close to him as the skin to an eel; during the day, he wore a marvelous vesture on which were painted leaves, spots of sun, dabs of blue shade, and stripes of earthy brown.

Now this Master Thief was no ordinary robber, for he stole not for stealing's sake, but only to gather new rarities for a wonderful museum he housed in the caverns under his dwelling. Surely there was never such a marvelous museum as the museum of the Master Thief!

Deep in the solemn echoing caves, ticketed and labeled each one, and arranged in order, shelf on shelf, was to be found the *finest specimen* of everything in the world which men had made or loved. The most comfortable chair in the world was there, the pointedest pin, the warmest blanket, the loudest drum, the stickiest glue, the most interesting book, the funniest joke, the largest diamond, the most lifelike stuffed cat, the handsomest lamp-shade, and a thousand things more. To relabel his collection, to move it about, to do things to it and with it was the supreme delight of the Master Thief. Seated in the most comfortable chair in the world, finger tips together, he spent hours gloating on his treasures, and wondering if he lacked aught beneath the sun. Presently he chanced to hear of the invisible baby's opal perambulator, and instantly determined to add this new wonder to his gallery.

Going first to his secret den, he spun for himself a globe of delicate glass, spoke five words into it, and sealed them snug within. Next, he attired himself in his parti-colored suit, put the globe in his pocket, and fled on his long legs over hill and over dale to the royal city.

Arriving late in the afternoon, he made his way without difficulty into the gardens of the palace. The day was fair as only a day on the threshold of summer may be, and the opal perambulator stood unattended in the shade of a clump of ancient trees. Magnificently clad, a number of royal nurses were standing about the silver fence which enclosed the prince's romping-yard. Far off, in the sunny distance, sounded the drums and fifes of the palace soldiery.

And now, creeping nearer unobserved, the Master Thief took the crystal globe from his pocket and tossed it near the group. Striking the ground, the globe burst with the faintest crystal tinkle, and the words that the cunning Master Thief had sealed within escaped into the air. And these words were: —

Oh, look at the balloon!

Immediately all the nurses looked to the sky to see the imaginary balloon, and while they were looking here and looking there, the Master Thief sprang to the opal perambulator, released the brake on the golden wheels, and, pushing the carriage ahead of him, ran like mad down the flower-bordered alleyways and out the garden gates to the highroad.

Across the landscape in a long straight line

Over hill, over dale, in a long straight line, fled the Master Thief with the golden perambulator

fled the Master Thief on his wonderful legs, pushing the perambulator all the while. Now they saw him bouncing it across furrowed fields, now they saw it speed like a jeweled boat through a sea of waving green grain, now they beheld it scattering the silly sheep in the upland wilds.

Presently the bells of the city set up the maddest ringing; foot soldiers were turned out on the roads, and squadrons of cavalry were sent galloping after; but all in vain — the jeweled carriage, blazing in the western glow, sped like a meteor over the land. The last they saw of it was a moving streak of light along the steep slope of a mountain, a light which gleamed for a moment on the crest like a large, misplaced, and iridescent star, and then swiftly sank from view.

When the Master Thief reached his secret haven in the valley, he shouted aloud for triumph, and swiftly wheeled the perambulator down to the museum. *The most magnificent perambulator in the world!* Once more drawing forth the most comfortable chair, the Master Thief sank into it and contemplated his newest prize.

Suddenly, a strange sound, half cry, half gurgle caused him to sit bolt upright. Had someone discovered his secret treasury? What could it mean? And now there came a second cry which ended in a long protesting wail.

The Master Thief had stolen the invisible baby along with the carriage!

Now the notion of having to take care of a baby, of any baby, was a matter which might well alarm the Master Thief; but as for an *invisible* baby, that was indeed a trial! All at once, however, the Master Thief slapped his knee and chuckled for joy — he had thought of the spell-dispeller! Holding aloft the brightest lantern in the world, the robber made his way to the little side-cavern in which he had placed the talisman.

His heart jumped. The spell-dispeller was gone!

Baffled and perplexed, the Master Thief began a nervous search of the little cavern; but never a sign of the spell-dispeller could he find. Vowing not to restore the Prince till he had found the talisman and tested its power, the Master Thief at length abandoned the search and carried the Prince through the caverns to his dwelling.

And now days passed, and months passed, and even years, without bringing to light the spell-dispeller. From an invisible infant the Prince grew to be an invisible boy, whose merry voice and friendly presence played about the house of the Master Thief like a capful of summer wind on a mountain lake.

Heigho, but after all it was n't so bad to be invisible! One could see things and find things hidden away from all other mortals; one could climb to the side of a bird's nest, sit still, and watch the mother bird feed her young; one could dive, unseen, into the clear, cold pools of the mountain streams and pinch the lurking trout by their rippling tails; one could follow the squirrel to his secret granary!

Now, during the Prince's fifteenth year, it came to pass that the Master Thief suddenly became ashamed of his wicked ways, so ashamed indeed that he resolved not only to forgo further *collecting* but also to return every single thing he had stolen! The invisible Prince, I am glad to tell you, was of the greatest possible service to the Master Thief in this honest task. And now, all over the kingdoms of the world, people began to find their stolen possessions waiting for them when they came down to breakfast in the morning: the stuffed cat became once more the pride of the Blue Tower, the most interesting book went back to its place on the shelves of the royal library, the golden scroll of the funniest joke appeared as if by magic on the wall of the king's own room. Alas for human waywardness, there were actually people who had grown so accustomed to the loss of their belongings that they reviled the Master Thief for their return. Dreadful to relate, — the style having changed, — the handsomest lamp-shade was actually tossed in a well!

At the end of the fifth year, the opal perambulator and the invisible Prince were the only two stolen things left to return. The invisible youth was twenty years old. With a sorrowful heart, for the youth was as dear to him as a son, the repentant Master Thief began preparations to restore prince and perambulator to the unhappy parents.

Now it came to pass that, on the morning of departure, the Master Thief descended for the last time to the forlorn and dusty corridors of his great museum and walked about the galleries, leaving footprints in the dust and musing on the glories that had been. Here had stood the shiniest rubber-plant, here the most beautiful hat-rack, here the only eraser which had never rubbed a hole in the paper. A tear gathered in his eye. He had loved them; he had stolen them; he had restored them; he was free!

All at once his glance, roving empty shelves, fell on a tiny box wedged in a sombre corner. With a loud shout of joy, the Master Thief recognized the spell-dispeller! It had fallen behind a shelf and had lain there concealed for almost twenty years! Thrusting it into his pocket's depth, the Master Thief bounded up the secret stairs to the joy of the sun.

After a pleasant rambling journey in a huge coach, the Master Thief and the invisible Prince reached the city at the twilight hour, and took lodgings at a quiet, comfortable inn. The invisible Prince, I must remind you, was still invisible.

Now it came to pass that when supper had been served and eaten, the Master Thief and the invisible Prince went for a stroll through the royal city. Much to the surprise of the travelers, they found the city hung with streamers and bunting of the gayest kind. Stranger still, in spite of this display, the citizens of the royal city appeared to be particularly out of spirits.

"Good host," said the Master Thief to the landlord of the inn, "pray what means this air of jubilee? Do you make merry for some kingly festival?"

"A festival, yes," replied the host, looking about to see if anyone were listening, "festival it is, but only in name. Have you not heard the news? Let us walk a little to one side and I will tell you the story.

"Three years ago our gracious sovereign, the good King Valdoro the Fourth — weary of the cares of state and still stricken to the heart by the loss of his son, the invisible Prince of whom you may have heard — gave over the guidance of the kingdom to the Marquis Malicorn. Last week this official made himself master of the royal power, imprisoned our dear King and Queen in a dark tower, and proclaimed himself successor to the throne. The coronation is to be held to-morrow afternoon in the great hall of the royal palace. Alas for the people and the nation! Oh, if the invisible Prince would only return!"

To this the Master Thief nodded his head, his busy brain plotting all the while. All at once he smiled. He had devised a plan.

And now it was once more the great hall of the castle, and once more a sunny afternoon. Bells rang, but their cry was wingless and leaden, and there was a dull and joyless note in the cannon's roar. Crowded as densely together as ever they were twenty years before, the magnificoes sullenly awaited the arrival of the usurper and his train.

Presently the portals were once more swept apart, revealing Malicorn and his followers. Not a sound rose from the assembly.

Growling for rage beneath a huge pair of dragoon's whiskers, the wicked Marquis made his way to the dais and the coronation chair. The noise of bells and cannon ceased. An official in blue advanced with the royal robe.

Just as he was about to throw it over the waiting shoulders of the usurper, an invisible something snatched the robe from him and, lo, it melted into the air!

Exceedingly angry, yet disturbed at heart, Malicorn hoped for better luck with the sceptre, but this, too, was snatched by an invisible hand. As for the royal crown, it vanished from its purple cushion in the twinkling of an eye.

Speechless with rage, Malicorn now rose to his feet, and stood before the throne, glaring about into the air. Cries of defiance, mingled with shouts of derision, rose from among the magnificoes. And now, even as the turmoil was at its height, the Master Thief, who had been concealed behind some curtains, strode boldly forth to the dais, thrust Malicorn aside with a sweep of his long arms, and shouted to the audience: —

"Magnificoes of the Realm, you came to see your King. Your rightful King is here. Would you behold him?"

"Yes!" shouted the assembly in one voice. And now the Master Thief touched the invisible Prince with the spell-dispeller.

The instant he did so a flash of deep golden light set everyone blinking, fairy music was heard, and suddenly the invisible Prince stood visible before the throne. He was tall, dark-haired, brown-eyed, and a bit slim, and the crown was on his head, the robe on his shoulders, and the sceptre in his hand.

And now the bells and cannon began to boom in real earnest, and a gay breeze came sweeping in to toss the flags and banners that had hung so still. Overcome by emotion, the generalissimo seized the Lord Chancellor by the waist and swung him into a jig, the soldiers all tossed their caps into the air and cheered like mad, whilst the organist became so excited that he began to play two tunes at once. Everybody was laughing and hallooing and hurrahing.

As for Malicorn and his crew, they were tumbling out the back door as fast as their legs could carry them, and nobody has seen them from that day to this.

Presently the old King and the Queen, released from the dark tower, came hurrying in to greet their son.

"He resembles you, my dear," whispered the King to the Queen.

The Master Thief was forgiven everything.

Singing and rejoicing, the people of the city poured from the houses into the sunny streets.

Clang, clang! Boom! Clang, clang! Boom, boom! Boom! Boom!

And they all lived happily ever after.

THE TWO MILLERS

ONCE upon a time, in a pleasant country of meadows sweeping seaward from wooded inland heights, there were two millers and two mills. If you came to the country in a ship, you saw the windmill first, for it was built upon a tongue of land rising above the wide salt meadows and the washing midnight-tides; but if you came to the country by the land, it was the water mill you saw, for it stood beside the highway in the valley of a brooklet rushing to the sea.

Now the wind-miller, who was a great tall man with blue eyes and fair hair, had a daughter named Cecily, whilst the water-miller, who was a little nimble man with a red face and crisp, black curls, had a son named Valentine. And because both the millers were merry men, and there was a plenty of grain for both the mills to grind, these millers were excellent cronies, and the maiden Cecily had been betrothed to the young man Valentine.

Every eve, when the day's task at the water mill had been brought to an end, the gates lowered, and the brooklet turned free to rush unhindered down the glen, Valentine would walk from his wooded hills to the headland by the sea, and call at the mill for Cecily. The nights were often still, and the golden shield of the moon, rising over the hilly woods, gleamed upon the curling foam of the little long waves, and filled their glassy hollows with her light.

Now it befell that as Valentine and Cecily walked by the shore on such a night, they heard from the hollow of the hills a faint and far-off rumble like the echoing of thunder. Such mysterious sounds were forever rising in the hills, and because no one could tell whence they came, a legend had grown up that somewhere in the forest depths there dwelt a hidden someone, known as the Husbandman of the Hills.

"Listen, Valentine," said Cecily, "the Husbandman of the Hills is closing the door of his barn. Think you that some day a mortal may find him in his hiding-place in the hills?"

"But suppose it were naught but an idle tale?" said the merry youth, with a smile.

"Oh no, Valentine," said the maiden seriously. "All my life long have I dwelt here on the shore, and heard the mysterious echoes from the hills. Sometimes the sound is of the lowing of cattle, sometimes of the threshing of grain, sometimes 't is the creaking of a hay wain in a field. And always the old and wise tell of the Husbandman of the Hills. Some day a mortal will find the hidden Husbandman — do you but wait and see."

It was the early summer now, and all went merry as a marriage bell. The heavy water-wheel turned with a rolling thunder and a sound of endless splashing; and the four arms of the windmill spun with a windy thrum and a clock-like clack from the rising of the wind to the calm of sundown and the eve.

And now, alas, events were at hand which were to shatter the plans of the two millers and wreck the hopes of Cecily and Valentine!

At the close of the harvest-tide, the Princess Celestia, only daughter of the King and Queen of the country, was going to be married. Now it chanced that the Queen, her mother, was famous in the land as a maker of cake, and presently this good lady promised her daughter a wedding cake so splendid and delicious that painters would beg to be allowed to paint its portrait, and poets to praise it in glorious and immortal song.

Yes, the Queen would make the cake with her own white hands, the batter should be mixed in a golden bowl with a golden spoon, the two best hens in the kingdom should be summoned to lay the eggs, the oven should have a door of diamonds, and as for the flour, that should come from the finest fields and the best mill in all the land.

"I know what I 'll do; I 'll offer a rich reward

for the best flour," said the good Queen. And calling the royal herald to her presence, she bade him summon all good millers to strive for the prize, and to bring of their new flour to the palace at the close of the harvest yield.

Now it chanced that the Queen's herald, all dressed in blue-and-white and sounding a silver horn, came cantering first to the water-miller's door.

"I should like to win that treasure," said the water-miller to himself, musing in the doorway. "After all, my flour *is* better than the wind-miller's meal. That treasure should be mine, must be mine. Yes, mine, mine, mine!"

Now it was the custom of the country for millers to visit the farms in midsummer, view the growing, green grain, and bargain with the husbandmen for the yield of the tossing fields. Suddenly the water-miller, coveting the treasure, determined to purchase all the standing grain, so that the wind-miller should not have any good grain to grind! And this he did, forgetting the while that the deed was sharp and unfriendly.

A day or two passed, and presently the wind-miller climbed to the saddle of his fat white steed, and rode away to buy his customary grain. Alas, there was none to be had. Every turn of the road disclosed new fields of grain, but every single ear was pledged to the miller by the brook!

At first — I must tell you — the wind-miller was more hurt than angry at his old crony's trickery; but the more he thought of it the angrier he grew. Storming about the windmill in a rage, he gave a great roar for Cecily, and when the frightened maiden appeared before him, he bade her dismiss all thoughts of Valentine from her heart, and consider herself fortunate to be rid of the son of such a father.

The water-miller, however, was not to be outdone. The moment he heard of the wind-miller's wrath, he too fell into a rage, and presently forbade Valentine, on pain of dismissal, so much as to look at the maiden Cecily.

And now the youth and the maiden were very sad indeed, for in spite of the strife between their fathers, they continued to love each other very much. Presently Valentine could endure it all no more, and stole away one night to have a word with Cecily.

The mill brook was babbling in the dark when Valentine returned to the mill, and a single light was burning in a window by the door. Opening the portal gently, the youth presently discovered his father seated on the stair clad in a flowered nightcap and a long white dressing-gown.

"Valentine," said the water-miller in a voice deep as the bottom of a well, "where have you been?"

"I 've been to the windmill to see Cecily," said Valentine truthfully and bravely.

"Sirrah!" cried the water-miller, shaking with such temper that his flowered nightcap trembled on his head. "Did I not forbid you to go to the windmill, on pain of being turned away from this my house? Go!" And the angry water-miller pointed a level finger out into the night.

"But, father," protested Valentine.

"But me no buts," thundered the miller. "Go, sirrah, for this house is yours no more."

"But whither, father?" asked bewildered Valentine.

"That, sirrah, is your affair," replied the angry miller. "Go anywhere you please; go find the Husbandman of the Hills!"

And with this last bit of advice, the wrathful water-miller pushed his son out of the mill and drew the long, grinding bolt across the door. A moment later the single light went out, and the mill was dark.

And now Valentine, in search of shelter for the night, sought out a farm in the gloom of the wooded hills. Leaving the broad white road, he followed first a country lane, then a pathway winding through a great woodsy mire, and then another lane, softly carpeted with moss and last year's fallen leaves.

A star fell from the twinkling heavens; a hunting owl hooted in a tree. Ever so far away a silver bell struck the midnight hour.

Suddenly Valentine knew that he had followed a strange path, and was lost in the heart of the hills. It was a very strange path indeed, for the trees and the brambles along it seemed to have grown together in the dark, and pressed forward to form a thick imprisoning wall.

Uneasy at heart, the youth now turned to retrace his steps, only to see that the same mysterious trees had risen up behind!

Hours passed. Stars that were high in the heavens vanished over treetops in the east, a silvery dawn began to pale, and there were chirps and stirs and peeps and feathery noises in the wood. At the rising of the sun, Valentine arrived at the farm of the Husbandman of the Hills.

Now the Husbandman of the Hills — I must

tell you — was the farmer of the fairies. It was from this farm in the hills that the goblins of the mountain-tops, the elves of the silver river, and the peoples of the fairy kingdoms of the world had their apples and clotted cream, their cherries and plums, and their butter-pats stamped with a crown.

The fairy farm lay in a green vale, magically walled about with briery trees. Only at the midnight minute could the wall be passed, and Valentine had chanced to cross it at the sixth stroke of the bell.

And now Valentine found himself made welcome by the Husbandman and his lady, the Goodwife of the Hills. The Husbandman was old; his face was ruddy and his hair silvery white, and in a smock of blue with a white collar was he clad. His spouse was elderly too, and wore a gown of green with short old-fashioned sleeves, a white housekeeper's-apron, and a cap with ribbons and frills.

I wish I had time to tell you of how the long

summer passed at the farm of the fairies — of the brewing, the baking, and the churning; and of how the green elves came to cut the grain with silver scythes no longer than your arm; of how a very young giant, who had a pleasant smile and was as tall as a tree, came to pitch the hay into the barn; of how the orchard goblins came to gather the wonderful apples into baskets of silver and gold; and of the enchanted bear who wore yellow spectacles and turned the butter churn.

Presently the leaves, though green, began to rustle dryly on the trees, and Valentine began to long for his own again.

"You have been a faithful laborer," said the old Husbandman of the Hills. "A reward is yours. What shall it be?"

"But I seek no reward," said Valentine, "for you gave me shelter, when shelter I had none."

"A brave answer," said the old Husbandman with a smile. "But you have earned your wage, good friend. I 'll give you *a wish.* Be in no haste to use it. And guard it well!"

And now Valentine turned from the vale, passed the magic bound at midnight, and found himself once more in an old, familiar pathway of the wood.

The autumn had been a rainless one, and the water-miller was having forty fits.

The mill brook was running dry!

Already there was scarce water enough to stir the heavy wheel. Another week without rain, and the bed of the brook would be naught but a length of puddles and pools. And the fine golden grain he had purchased was being threshed and winnowed, and would soon be arriving at the mill!

In and out of the door of the mill, a hundred times a day went the water-miller, now to stare at the vanishing brook, now to sweep the sky in hope of rain. But the dry leaves only rustled more dryly, and the sun was bright.

Worse yet, the Princess Celestia's wedding

day was fast approaching, and the Queen would soon be calling for her flour. And sure enough, the Queen's herald presently rode again through the land, summoning all good millers to bring of their new flour to the palace before sundown on the seventh day.

The following week was indeed an anxious one for the miller by the brook. Alas for his fortunes — not a single drop of rain fell either in the meadows or the hills, and the brook ran dry. You might as well have tried to turn the wheel with a pitcher of water as to turn it with the trickle which remained.

On the night of the sixth day, the water-miller, humbled in heart, rode over to the wind-mill to make his peace and ask a boon. He would ask the wind-miller to grind the wonderful golden grain, and offer him half of the grain as a reward.

Now the wind-miller had not forgotten the water-miller's trickery; so he received his old crony with anything but a friendly air.

"Grind grain for you, sir?" said the windmiller, standing with arms akimbo and feet apart, "yes, sir; but only on one condition, sir, and that is, sir, that you let me choose my half of the grain, sir.

"And hearken, sir, one thing more, sir. You must bring the grain to the windmill this very night, sir."

Now it came to pass that, as the water-miller, hanging his head, went out into the night, Cecily saw him, and ran to ask him for news of Valentine. But the water-miller was himself troubled because of the absence of his son, and could give no new tidings to the maid.

Groaning many a regretful groan, the water-miller loaded his fine two-wheeled scarlet cart with sacks of golden grain, and carried it to the windmill door. It was a warm night. The water-miller unloaded the sacks, mopped his brow with a red bandanna handkerchief, and sighed.

What a fool he had been not to play fair! What a fool to send away his son!

When the water-miller had driven away, the triumphant wind-miller took a great iron lantern, and went down to see the grain. For a moment or two he stood motionless, chuckling at his unexpected victory. Presently he called to Cecily to gather all the lights and candles she could find, and place them round about.

And now, toiling in a great blaze of candle-light, the wind-miller slowly and carefully sifted out for himself the better half of the wonderful grain. The remaining half — which was good enough, but full of husks and dust — he set apart for his rival.

The dawn was breaking as he finished the task. Some of the candles were burned out, and the lanterns were smoke-begrimed and dim. Wearily rubbing the grain-dust from his eyes, the wind-miller trudged up the circular stair and tumbled into bed. He would grind the grain into flour as soon as he woke in the morn.

And on that same still, autumn dawn young Valentine came out of the fairy wood.

When the wind-miller woke, he woke with a start, for he had slept late, and the sun was high. How warm and misty-moisty it was! Good heavens — there was n't a breath of wind!

A ship drifted becalmed upon the glassy sea; a blue haze of wavy summer heat lay upon the meadows, and over the wooded hills hung a motionless mass of bluish cloud with a rim of silvery white. There was not even air enough to stir a dead leaf hanging by a thread.

In and out of the door of the mill, like one distracted ran the miller; he stood upon the balcony and stared about at the sky, the greeny-leaden sea, and the helpless ship; he lifted a moistened finger to the air.

Oh, for a wind!

And now a ship's bell in the mill struck the eight strokes of high noon, and presently the water-miller came hurrying to the mill in his scarlet cart. A moment's glance at the two halves of golden grain told him of the wind-

He lifted a moistened finger to the air. Good heavens — there was n't a breath of wind!

miller's counterstroke, and he ran upstairs into the mill room full of wrath.

"I brought you my grain to grind," he shouted at the wind-miller, "and you have not done so. I shall take it all back again, do you hear?"

"Wait; you made a bargain with me," answered the wind-miller.

"I tell you I am done with the bargain," cried out the water-miller in a passion.

"I tell you a bargain 's a bargain," shouted the wind-miller. "Touch yon grain if you dare!"

And now, I am sure, the old friends and cronies would have come to blows, had not Valentine and Cecily suddenly hurried and rushed between them.

"Good sirs," said honest Valentine, "pray you stand apart and do each other no wrong. The brook is dry; the wind is gone; of what use then is this disputed grain? Were it not best, mayhap, to begin anew?"

"Dear father," said pretty Cecily, "Will you give your share of the grain to me?"

"With all my heart," said the wind-miller, who hated brawling.

"And will you give your share to me, father?" asked Valentine.

"Yes, and gladly," said the water-miller.

"Heart's thanks to you both, good sirs," said the youth with a bow and the maid with a courtesy. "And now," continued Valentine, "you shall all behold a great wonder.

"O Husbandman of the Hills, you gave me a wish for a wage. Grant it to me now! I wish for a fine windmill-wind to blow till sundown of this day."

Out of the hills came the wind. It swept up an inland dust, it sent the leaves on the higher crests a-flying, it rushed over the hot sea-scented meadows, it surged about the mill — and the great arms gathered it, creaked, groaned, and began a-spinning.

Valentine poured a shower of grain down an oaken slide into the grinding thunder of the heavy stones. The grain fell between the upper and the nether wheel, and presently the finest of new flour was pouring down below. And this new flour the three millers shook and sifted and cleansed until it was worthy of the Queen's own hands, the golden batter-bowl, and the Princess Celestia's cake. So wonderful indeed was the flour, that it instantly gained the rich reward the Queen had offered as a prize, and won for Valentine the appointment of miller to the King.

Touched by the happiness of their children, I am glad to say, the two millers agreed to forget their strife. And they shook hands, and became cronies again.

On the day following the wedding of the Princess Celestia, Valentine and Cecily were married. The little Princess sent them two thick slices of her cake. It was as white as snow, and frosted with sugar, and there were candied plums, and cherries, and citron nibbles in each slice.

And Valentine and Cecily rejoiced, and lived happily together all their days.

THE ADAMANT DOOR

ONCE upon a time, on a fine spring morning, a country lad named Hugh took his fish pole from a corner and went to try his luck in a brook beside the road. Now it fortuned that as he stood upon the grassy bank, casting about in the broad shallows of the stream, the boy heard the mighty sound of many men singing together, and presently he beheld a regiment of soldiers on the march. In uniforms of red-and-white they were clad, and an officer in red-and-white and gold was riding at their head.

And now the regiment came to a halt, and broke ranks beside the brook. With shouts and cries the young soldiers hurried to the water, opened their gay coats at the throat, and washed the dust from their sunburnt faces; the sergeants gathered and gossiped by themselves; the horse of the guiding officer sucked up great mouths of water, looked about, and blew the spray from his nostrils; and here and there a man helped a comrade with his pack.

"How splendid it must be to be a soldier!" thought Hugh as he gazed upon the merry company. And, hurrying home to his mother as fast as his legs could carry him, he begged so eagerly for permission to enlist, that at length he won her consent and followed the marching men.

And now the lad Hugh was himself a soldier of the realm with a red-and-white uniform like unto the others, a pack for his back, and a shiny leather hat with a shiny silver star. Soon he knew what it was to lie upon the ground and shiver in a blanket, and to watch the rolling stars, and hear the night wind cry.

Now it chanced that there was another young soldier of Hugh's age enlisted in the company, and with this lad, whose name was Jocelyn, Hugh presently became the best of friends. This Jocelyn was a mountaineer and was slender and yellow-haired; whilst Hugh was a lad of the plain and was sturdy of frame and dark. And because these two lads were the youngest of the company and were loyal friends, they marched down the highway side by side and shared together the good and ill of life.

Now it came to pass upon a summer's night, as the soldiers lay encamped in fields by the royal city, that the great bell of the King's palace broke the quiet of the stars with a loud and unending clangor of alarm. It was late, the watch fires had almost burned away, and the soldiers, waking in the dark, seized upon their arms and wondered at the din. All at once, with a thunder of hoofs, a messenger from the city came spurring in with the news that war was at hand, and that the regiment must break camp on the instant and speed to the borders of the realm. Presently fresh branches tossed upon the embers filled the camp with the light of flames, and bugle calls rang through the tumult and the clanging of the bell.

Left! Right! Left! Right! And the soldiers were marching to the wars. They came to ancient hamlets in the night, and found soldiers of other companies already sleeping in the barns; they marched through lonely forests, and warmed their noonday meal with a blaze of twigs and fallen boughs; they marched singing through the fields of golden grain. Soon the villages and the fields grew rare, a silence fell upon the land, and the regiment found itself at the edge of a vast and lonely moor. Regiments without number were there encamped, and their bivouac fires gleamed at night like a thousand scattered stars.

Leagues away, on barren hills rising to the north, were to be seen the fires of the foe.

And now it was the morn of battle: a red sun was rising above the brown hills and hollows of the moor, the air was sluggish, and flat gray clouds lay motionless and low. Tarantara! Tarantara! went the bugles, regiment after regiment came marching to its post, the plain shook to the tramp of feet, the horsemen gathered behind, the drums began to sound, the men in red-and-white marched down to the moor, and presently the great hollow of the waste rang like a brazen cup with the beginning tumult of the fray.

The soldiers of the enemy were clad in black-and-white, and wore shiny leather hats with shiny golden stars.

The young comrades marched into battle side by side. And even as a branch, thrust gently from the bank of a racing river, first moves slowly in calm waters by the edge of the stream and then is caught up and tossed about by the wild mid-torrent, so did the great tide of the battle catch up Jocelyn and Hugh. They fought as in a dream, scarce knowing what they did.

Now it came to pass that, at the storming of a grassy hillock of the moor, Hugh was taken prisoner by the men in black-and-white, but was bravely rescued by Jocelyn who fought his way undaunted to his side. Presently the enemy yielded the disputed hill, and the company in red-and-white made ready to hold it for their own.

The day waned; a tide of dark and threatening cloud rose over the horizon to the east, and a cold wind rode before it, bringing rain. All at once a wild and terrible storm burst over the battle on the moor; and, under cover of the thunder and confusion, the men in black-and-white strove to regain the hillock for their own. A bellowing wind whipped the heavy rain in the soldiers' eyes, and it was very hard to see.

Now it fortuned that, in the dark of the storm and the tumult of the fray, the boy Hugh became separated from his comrades and suddenly found himself out of the battle, and wandering quite alone. Night was rushing on, the din of the combat was muffled in the roaring of the rain, and the young soldier scarce knew where to go.

Now it was his duty to return to the battle, seek out his comrades, and fight beside them to the end. Alas, so weary and shaken was the soldier lad that he made no effort to return to his hard-pressed friends, but fled away from the battle through the dark! Presently the all but roofless ruin of a shepherd's hut appeared ahead, and Hugh took refuge within it from the battle and the storm.

All night long he lay there on the stones of the floor, sunken in a shivering sleep; but the dawn woke him at last, and he crept to a window to look forth upon the moor.

All was still. The battle was lost. The men in black-and-white were encamped upon the nearer hillocks of the moor, and a company of their horse was guarding a square of some hundred men in white-and-red.

Suddenly the runaway soldier heard the beat of a distant drum and, gazing through a cranny of the ruined house, beheld a number of prisoners marching by, forlorn. A triumphant dragoon in black-and-white was riding at their head; the drummer of his own company

followed close behind, mournfully beating his drum; and then, trudging wearily on, appeared the good comrades whom he had deserted in their need. And Jocelyn walked among them bareheaded, with his arms tied behind him at the wrist.

And now the dark waters of sorrow and shame welled up in the heart of the runaway soldier, and he wept bitterly that he had failed to return into the fray. He would have leaped from the house and taken his place with his comrades, save that he could not bear that they should know of his flight.

Now it came to pass, when the drum-beats had faded into the silence of the moor, that Hugh discovered a shepherd's smock and wide-brimmed hat hanging on a peg, and abandoned his uniform for these. Thus clad, he fled from the hut in the dead of night and made his escape across the moor. Because of the triumph of the enemy, he dared not return into his own land, but fled to a kingdom in the west.

Presently he came upon a village lying at the foot of a hill crowned with a ruined tower, and there took service in the harvest fields.

As for Jocelyn and his comrades, they were marched into the enemy's country, thrust into dungeons, and held for ransom, one and all.

Now it fortuned that one noontide, as Hugh rested with fellow laborers in the greenwood shade, he asked them of the ruined castle on the hill.

"Yon castle," said a big harvester with an important air, "was built centuries ago by an old knight who was known throughout the land as a magician. A treasure lies hid within, but none dare seek it; for those who do —"

"Never come back!" croaked another harvester, a little lean man with thin legs and large red ears.

"Once there was a brave adventurer who went to seek the treasure," said a man with long, uncut locks and a pointed nose. "We watched him climb the hill, we saw him enter the castle, and all at once we heard — "

"A terrible yell!" said the big harvester and the red-eared man together.

"And he never came back," said somebody else, shaking his head.

"Bless us," cried Hugh, "but what do you suppose it is that guards the treasure?"

"Well, if you ask me, I 'll tell you," said the big harvester; "it 's a trigorgon."

"A trigorgon?" questioned Hugh. "And pray, sir, what is a trigorgon?"

"A trigorgon is a creature that has only three legs," continued the big harvester. "It 's triangular and flattish, the one leg being at the front under the long neck, the two legs riding behind. Short, thick, elephant-like legs, body like a turtle, double rows of teeth, violent disposition. I 've read of it in a book."

"Bother your book," cried red-ears. "The trigorgon you describe, my good sir, is quite impossible. A trigorgon has its two legs in front, and its one leg behind. A neck has got to have shoulders to rest on, has n't it? You see, young man, the trigorgon uses its one hind leg to push itself ahead at a frightful speed. I know!"

"How do you know?" asked the big harvester with some displeasure.

"Because the seventh son of a seventh son's great-grandmother told me!" exclaimed red-ears triumphantly.

"Bother your seventh son's great-grandmother!" shouted the big harvester. "Now, my book had large print and most wonderful pictures!"

"Pish!" said red-ears.

"Tush for you and your seventh son of a seventh son's great-gran — "

"My friends! My friends!" interposed pointed-nose. "Why quarrel over this absurd trigorgon? You are both wrong. The castle is haunted by a thith, a terribly, dangerous thith. All over the land they say it 's a thith."

"Who say?" questioned the big harvester.

"They say," replied pointed-nose.

"Bother they, and all they say," shouted the big harvester, forgetting his grammar. "It 's a trigorgon!"

"It 's a thith!" shrieked pointed-nose.

And now began a tremendous uproar in which everybody took part, some agreeing with the big harvester, some with red-ears, and some with pointed-nose. A few who disbelieved in both the trigorgon and the thith stood disdainfully to one side, but suddenly they too began to quarrel violently among themselves as to whether the castle was haunted by a mistophant, a winged bogus, a bristly whiskeroarer or an ugsome vrish. So bitter grew the strife that presently red-ears and pointed-nose fell to fisticuffs and were separated with great difficulty by their fellow-harvesters.

"A treasure!" said Hugh to himself. "Ah, if I could but find it, I would ransom Jocelyn and the comrades." And with an uneasy heart, he thought of the trigorgon, the thith, the winged bogus, the snarling whiskeroarer, the mistophant, and the vrish.

How terrible it would be to meet creatures so awful that no human being had dared to see them! But Jocelyn and the comrades whom he had failed in their hour of peril on the moor, what of them? They were prisoners in the land of the foe; with the treasure of the castle he could ransom them — was he to fail them again?

All at once the runaway young soldier threw back his shoulders bravely and lifted his eyes to the sky. He would seek the treasure on the morrow's morn.

The sun was shining brightly, a cold dew was still glistening on the leaves, and the villagers had gathered by the public well to speed Hugh on his way. Shaking their heads doubtfully and mournfully, they watched him go swinging down the road and disappear into the trees upon the hill. Presently the glint of his blue smock began to be seen here and there along the climbing path, close by the summit of the mount. A little anxious time passed, and suddenly there rang from the ruin a long, wild howl.

"There, the trigorgon has got him," said the big harvester.

"You mean the giant thith," pointed-nose corrected.

I am glad to tell you, however, that they were both wrong. This is what had happened at the ruin.

Now Hugh had carried an ancient lantern with him from the village, and halfway up the hill he paused, cut a likely branch from an ash, and fashioned himself a stout and serviceable staff. Thus armed, he arrived at the great gate of the ruin, and forced his way through the thorn trees by the portal into the roofless square of the walls. There were trees there, too, and though the leaves were still green, every now and then one went drifting through the silence to the ground. In the heart of the wooded court, a broad flight of steps, overgrown with moss and shrubs of shallow root, led down into a darkness far below.

Grasping his cudgel firmly, Hugh descended the woodsy stair. The sunlight disappeared behind, the green moss grew no more, and clumps of leathery toadstools burst from the muddy crannies of the stone. Suddenly the runaway soldier found himself facing a giant pointed door of blackest adamant. Over the arch of it, in letters of ancient form, was carved a legend saying:—

He who would share the treasure
must conquer a mighty foe within

Behind the door something was roaring and roaring. "'T is surely the trigorgon," thought Hugh, his heart pounding at his ribs. Summoning up all his courage, the runaway soldier threw back the adamant door.

The instant he did so, the roaring rose to a

howling shriek, and a gust of the storm wind, magically imprisoned in the caves of the hill, went whistling out of the adamant door and up the tunnel of the stairway to the sun. It was this cry of the imprisoned gust which had made them shake their heads in the village below.

And now Hugh bravely set foot into the darkness and, holding his twinkling light at arm's length ahead, advanced to meet the mighty foe within. Through great halls he fared, and heard queer noises which he took to be the steps of the trigorgon, but were only the echoes of his own steps tapping in the dark; through long tunnels he trod, and heard breathings and whispers which he took to be the sighs of the thith, but were only the echoes of a chuckling brook, flowing somewhere in the wall. On and on went Hugh, and laughed a little to himself when he mistook two shining points of stone for the eyes of the winged bogus, and a monstrous round rock for the bulk of the mistophant.

Summoning up all his courage, Hugh threw open the adamant door

After a while, I am glad to tell you, he even ceased turning around now and then to see if he were being followed by the whiskeroarer or the vrish.

Presently Hugh began to hear the queerest tinkling-clinking ringing sound, unbroken in its flow as the trilling of a stream. A moment later the youth opened a second pointed door and stood in a lighted chamber, staring at a *fountain of money.*

The chamber was high and square; its roof and walls were of blackest adamant, twinkly-bright with specks of yellow gold, and a magic, ever-burning lamp of adamant hung from above, yielding a golden light. In the height of the further wall a great fountain-like opening there was, framed in a golden star, and through this there poured a ringing cataract of coins of yellow gold! Below the shower of money, a semicircular basin, raised above the floor on pillars strangely carved, received the golden flood and lay full to the brim of clinking pieces of gold rising, falling, tossing, and washing about like waters in a pool. About the brim of the fountain there ran a sculptured band of stone whereon men were shown engaged in honorable labor — the farmer scattered the seed, the harvester gathered the grain, the smith labored at his forge, and a master workman carved a fair statue from a block of faultless stone.

And Hugh, pausing to look at the pieces of gold, saw that they were of ancient years and sealed with the seal of old, forgotten kings.

Now it came to pass that, when Hugh had filled his pockets and his hat with gold, he discovered a third adamant door leading from the chamber and, passing through it, found himself blinking in the sunlight on the further side of the hill. Strange to say, in the wall of stone behind him there was never a sign or appearance of a door!

But the mighty foe within — what could it be? He had seen nothing of the trigorgon, the thith, the winged bogus, the whiskeroarer, the mistophant, or the vrish. Yet the inscription had said that he must conquer a foe. Suddenly Hugh threw his hands into the air with a great merry shout; he had found the key to the mystery.

It was all a wise jest of the old knight. The foe to be conquered was fear, and "the mighty foe within" meant the host of silly fears which run and hide in the house of one's heart. The treasure had been guarded against men by their own fears. Brave men, who sent fears hurrying and scurrying out of their hearts, alone were worthy of the prize.

As for the trigorgon, the thith, the winged bogus, the whiskeroarer, the mistophant, and the ugsome vrish, they had never existed, for they were not creatures, but silly, thoughtless imaginings and fears.

And now Hugh, with his pockets laden with gold, walked over the hills to the enemy's land, and ransomed his comrade Jocelyn and the dear friends with whom he had marched to battle on the moor.

Presently a just and mighty emperor compelled both kingdoms to make peace, and the men in red-and-white and the men in black-and-white went home to their fields and their dear ones gathered by the fire.

And Hugh and Jocelyn shared the treasure together, and their farms lay side by side.

THE CITY OF THE WINTER SLEEP

ONCE upon a time, by the banks of a noble river flowing to the sea through a mountain-girdled plain, stood a city of the wisest people in the world. Instead of spending the winter as others did, huddled over smoky fires, freezing ears and noses, bundling themselves up in a pother of clothes, and being cross at breakfast, these sensible folk simply retired to their dwellings, locked their doors, drew down their curtains, put on their nightcaps, got into bed, and *slept the winter away*. The north wind howled there about the shuttered houses and woke no citizen from his dreams; in the empty market place and the silent streets, stainless and untrodden lay the snow. But when the leaves were the size of a mouse's ear, and the singing birds had returned from their winter pilgrimage, the sleepy citizens would wake, rub their eyes, stretch their arms, and come yawning to open their windows on the sunlight and the spring.

The King of this remarkable city, I must tell you, had three children, the two elder of whom were sons and the youngest a daughter. Now, as occasionally happens, the two sons were models of royal deportment, whilst their sister, the slender, dark-haired, and dark-eyed Princess Theolette, was as wilful and spirited as a mountain bird.

Now, on a day when the year was growing old and only a few half-withered flowers were to be gathered in the fields, it chanced that Theolette, who had been idling about with little to do, took it into her head to pay a visit to the royal library. It was very quiet there, the red autumn sun was shining through the great windows, a million motes of dust danced in the broad and ruddy beam, and Theolette, curled in a huge red-leather easy-chair, had great difficulty in keeping awake. Presently her eyes lit upon a large green book entitled, *Winter Time,* and this Theolette took from its place and opened in her lap.

Somewhat to her disappointment, the print within the old book was in a foreign language, but the pictures — they would have kept anyone from sleeping! There were pictures of snowy mountain-tops, of bright, frozen lakes with people skating on them, of attacks on snow forts, of snowstorms in pleasant country villages, and of belfries agleam with snow beneath the moon. Now, although Theolette had never seen the winter or any snow or ice and could hardly make anything out of some of the pictures, she could see well enough that here was something strange, and new, and wonderful indeed. And then and there she resolved to run away during the winter sleep, see the winter world, and return before the city woke to the coming of the spring!

Shorter grew the golden days, and longer the still cold nights, and presently the great day of the winter sleep was at hand. A trumpeter, posted in the tower of dreams, at sunrise called the city to its last morn of waking life; and scarce had his last notes faded, ere a murmur of bustle and preparations began to rise from every household in the town.

At sunset, in accordance with ancient custom, the edict of sleep was read to the people from a balcony of the palace. This venerable law, I must tell you, summoned all good citizens to go to sleep, and recited the dreadful penalties prepared for all who should dare to stay awake. When the gathering had melted away, and the streets were empty save for a hurrying citizen or two on some belated errand, the gates were locked and the waters of the river turned into the moat about the town.

The enchanted chimes of sleep, which rang of themselves, were to sound at the midnight hour.

Little by little, the royal palace became as silent as a stone. A darkness of slumber and night filled the vast echoing halls, and from afar through the gloom came the faint tramp, tramp of the hob-nailed night-watch on the last round of the year.

After attending the ceremonial winter good-night of the royal family, Theolette hurried away to her own chamber.

"I must n't fall asleep now," said she, clenching her fist, "because if I do, I 'll sleep until the spring!" And with a heart that went thump, thump, thump in the darkness, she waited the midnight hour.

Suddenly the first warning bell — *Nightcaps On!* — struck one great solemn rolling clang which swept out over the city and ebbed away humming to the stars.

And now, after a pause, sounded the second bell — *Lights out!* Theolette sat down in a great chair, arose, walked about, sat down again, and arose once more. Would the third bell never ring?

Presently — *Everybody to bed!* — boomed the

third bell. Theolette put her fingers to her ears. Solemn and sweet and strange and golden, the enchanted chimes were sounding their fairy tune.

Now, once the song of the chimes had come to an end and the throbbing humming of the last grave chord had melted into the air, Theolette went to her window, drew back the curtain, and looked forth over the city sleeping in the starlight. How strange and still they were, those dark streets winding like crooked brooks through banks of huddled roofs. Suddenly the Princess uttered a little cry of surprise!

Far away across the sleeping city, in a little house by the wall, a yellow light was gleaming! And now the light moved, went from window to window, vanished, reappeared, and vanished yet again.

Someone else was awake in the city! Who could it be?

Puzzled, but not the littlest bit afraid, the Princess went to her wardrobe and dressed herself as well as she could in a little red hunting-dress and cap. Then, throwing her warmest mantle over her shoulders and taking a lighted candle with her, she made her way from her chamber down the great stairway to the palace door. Fantastic shadows leaped and swayed as the Princess, holding aloft her taper, descended the long broad flight, and somewhere a huge clock ticked on, solemn, dutiful, and forgotten. Opening the door gently, Theolette stepped forth into the dark street and hurried along it to the royal gate of the city wall.

All seemed well; the gates were locked, and the drawbridge of the moat was lifted high above the black and starry waters. Standing motionless for a moment in one of the shadowy nooks of the giant portal, Theolette listened for a footfall or a sound, but heard only the sigh of the night wind and the ripple of water in the moat. Reassured by the silence, the Princess lowered the drawbridge, unlocked the great gate with her father's own key, opened one vast

The runaway Princess stepped forth into the dark street and, taper in hand, hurried to the gate of the city wall

swinging door, locked it behind her, and walked off bravely into the dark and lonely land.

On the following morning, a little after the dawn, the Princess arrived at a country town just over the frontier of her father's realm, and there she sought out the inn and made preparations for her runaway winter-pilgrimage. From the host, a little white horse she purchased, and from the host's fourth son, who happened to be a tailor, a fine warm riding-habit of country wool. Thus clad, away into the winter world galloped the adventurous Theolette. Of what befell her, you soon shall hear.

And what a wonderful pilgrimage it was through the world of ice and snow! I wish I had time to tell you of all she saw and of all she did, of how the first snowstorm so pleased her that she almost lost her way in the whirl of the flakes, of her first look at a bit of ice, of her visit to the winter festival of the Fairy of the Snows, of how she danced the minuet at the polar bears' ball, and of how she rode Aldebaran, the skating horse, up and down the ice lakes of the wild. White as snow was this marvelous animal, and of blue leather edged with white were his saddle and bridle, whilst the skates he wore were of the blackest and shiniest adamant. You should have seen him skating o'er the lakes, now striking out with this hoof, now with that; his head held high, his long silky tail streaming in the wind. And Theolette thought, as she rode, of the old book in the royal library and of the City of the Winter Sleep far away, with the storm crying unheeded through its dream.

And now the winter waned, a venturesome bird or two returned to rock on budding twigs, the earth began to turn from brown to green, and Theolette knew that she must hasten back at once. Alas! one pleasant morning, as she was nearing the borders of her father's land, a band of robbers suddenly sprang at her out of a wood, bound her securely, and hurried her to their castle with the intention of demanding a ransom. Once there, they pushed the Princess roughly into a little cobwebby turret-chamber, slammed and locked the heavy oaken door behind her, and left her to her thoughts.

From her window in the turret, Theolette could see the highroad leading toward the castle through the wooded lowlands, and the broad winding stream of a mighty river — the very river, indeed, which flowed by the walls of the City of the Winter Sleep. With every warm and sunny hour the spring was driving old winter from the land, the scales of tree buds were unsealing, frogs were piping in tiny triumph from every marsh and pool, and there were pleasant earthy smells in the air.

"The spring awakening is surely close at hand," thought Theolette. "What *shall* I do?"

Now, one sunny morning as the disconsolate Princess walked to and fro in her little room, it came to pass that she heard from the road below a pleasant voice singing a strange old song of her own land. It was a song about a soldier who had fought in the wars and returned in the spring to plough the dear earth he had loved and defended. And, hearing the old song, Theolette uttered a joyful cry and ran to the window. A youth in a student's dress of green stood in the highroad directly under the window; he had heard the cry, and stood looking up at the sunny wall.

"Stay, good sir," cried Theolette, "and tell me who you are that sings a song of mine own land."

To this the pleasant youth replied that he was but a student who had stolen away from the City of Winter Sleep, and was even then hastening back lest his absence be discovered. And Theolette remembered the light she had seen in the old house by the city wall.

And now Theolette told the student of her adventures and begged of him to aid her. You may be sure that the student, who was a fine brave fellow, needed no second entreaty! Being a clever youth as well as a brave one, he skillfully managed to lure the robbers away from the castle that very eve, and fling a coiled rope to the Princess. And, hand over hand, with feet pressed close against the cord, down came the adventurous Theolette.

Now, one of the robbers, a small one, had ridden away with Theolette's little white horse, so the student hurried Theolette to the river bank where a boat lay waiting. Alas, the vessel was scarce large enough for a single passenger!

"See, Princess, the river is in flood," said the youth, "and you have but to step into this vessel and be carried swiftly to the city."

"But what of you, brave friend?" said Theolette. "You will be late now, and your flight from the city will be known."

"Do not fear, Princess," replied the student with a queer, half-merry smile. "There is still time, and I can make haste as well as any man. To tell you truth, I have never felt at home in the city, anyway. But enough of words.

Hasten, Lady Theolette, for the robbers will soon return."

And now Theolette found herself on the mighty river in the full hurly-burly of its springtide flood. On and on she swept through the night, league after league, now floating quietly over lowlands turned to lakes; now borne headlong with the torrent down valleys and ravines. Solitary and fugitive, one great star shone close above the distant peaks.

Just as the dawn was streaking the east with rose and gray, the Princess gained her father's city. The drawbridge was still lowered across the moat, the city was still sealed in its winter dream.

After thrusting the little boat once more forth into the full current of the river, Theolette ran to the palace and went to her own room. With a little sigh, she folded away the worn red hunting-dress and cap she had been wearing — the riding-habit of country wool had been left behind somewhere at the return of spring —

and crept into her little silken bed. So weary was she that scarce had her head touched the pillow ere she was sound asleep.

When she opened her eyes again, a whole day and a night had passed, the City had risen from the winter sleep, and her mother stood bending over her with an amused smile. Loud and clear and joyous the silver bells of the spring-awakening were ringing o'er the town.

"Good gracious, Theolette," said her mother, "but what a sleeper you are! I 've been shaking you for the last ten minutes. Get up now, that 's a dear, and wear your rose frock to the grand spring breakfast."

A little later Theolette, feeling just the tiniest bit bewildered, sat down to breakfast with her father the King, her mother the Queen, and the two Princes her brothers. And there, moved by an impulse of truth and courage — for, though wilful, Theolette was as faithful to high honor as a vowed knight — the Princess told them all the tale of her runaway adventures. To her surprise, she could win none of them to believe her story!

"You have been dreaming, Theolette," said her father, gravely shaking his head and reaching for a royal muffin. "But I called you myself!" exclaimed her mother, pausing from her royal marmalade. And as for Theolette's two brothers, they pretended that polite disbelief which young men find so delightfully irritating when teasing their sisters.

Weeks passed, spring followed winter into the cupboard of time, and Theolette could find no one to believe her story. Weary of insisting, and shaken by the unbelief of those about her, the Princess began to wonder in her own heart if it were not all a dream. Nothing remained of it all, and it was so like a dream!

Her head bowed low, her eyes full of doubt and memories, the Princess mused all day, and finally grew so pale that her royal parents became quite alarmed, and took counsel to send their daughter on a long visit to her aunt, the Queen of the Golden Mountain. On the morn of departure, Theolette walked to the great hall of state to say farewell.

"A dream, a dream; was it only a dream?" thought Theolette. And she saw again the winter world, and the polar bears' ball, with the candles burning in chandeliers of icicles, and the skating horse, and the pleasant youth in green who had saved her from the robbers. Could it have been only a dream? With a sigh and a doubting shake of her head, the Princess took her place at the head of her ladies and approached her father and mother.

And now, of a sudden, from the sunny street below the pillared window, a voice was heard singing. And the voice sang an old song of a soldier who had fought in the wars and returned in the spring to plough the dear earth he had loved and defended. A hush fell over the astounded assembly.

"Stop, I pray you!" cried Theolette, turning

pale as the new-fallen snow. "O hasten, good soldiers, and bring yon singer here before me!"

And now a group of guards rushed through the swinging doors to do her bidding. Presently they returned, bringing with them the student who had saved Theolette from the robbers! He was very pale, there were irons on his wrists, and two burly turnkeys, dressed in red and black, stood beside him. And, beholding Theolette, the poor youth drew in his breath with a start and met her gaze with strange eyes.

"Speak! What does this mean? Who is this fellow?" cried the King, rising from his throne.

"May it please Your Majesty," replied a turnkey, falling on one knee, "this youth is a student of the College of Dreams who disobeyed the edict of sleep and ran away from the city. He was captured as he tried to return after the spring awakening, brought before the Court of Dreams, and sentenced to pay the penalty. We were on our way with him to the dungeons under the river when the royal guards surrounded us and led us here. What is your will, O King?"

"My will is that the judgment be obeyed," replied the King. "Lead him forth to his doom!"

"Nay, hear me, father," cried Theolette. "If he is guilty, so am I! I, too, disobeyed the edict; I, too, ran away. This is the brave youth who so gallantly preserved me from the robbers! Oh, will you not believe me now? It is not a dream — it never was a dream!"

At these words, a stir of excitement swept through the vast hall; indeed, it seemed as if all there were trying to talk, to protest, to support, to dispute, to explain. The uproar was at its height when the boom of a cannon first quieted, then roused the hubbub to an even greater pitch.

"A royal visitor!" exclaimed the King. "What can this mean? Let no one stir!"

Presently, there was a fanfare of many trumpets, the great portals of the hall swung open, and there entered a crowned King and his train.

"O King of the City of the Winter Sleep," cried the newcomer, "hear me, for I have come from afar and in great haste. I am the King of the North and I seek my only son, Prince Florimond, who was stolen from his cradle twenty years ago. The Fairy of the Isles has revealed that I shall find him here. He dwells in a house by the city wall and is a student of the College of Dreams. I pray you search for him at once, for my heart hungers to behold him!"

"Florimond? Florimond?" cried the Lord Chancellor of the College, stepping forward, "there is but one Florimond in the city and, as I live, this youth is he!" And presently all beheld that the great King and the runaway student were indeed father and son. To pardon the runaway youth and loose him from his bonds was but a moment's task. This done, a royal herald proclaimed a three days' holiday.

On the last evening of the festival, Florimond and Theolette walked alone to a great balcony and looked forth over the city, the river, and the mountain-circled plain. It was midsummer eve, the warm night was sweet with the fragrance of many flowers, and the music of lutes and viols sounded faintly through the pleasant air.

"Was it a wonder that I ran away," said the Prince, laughing, "when I was n't born a winter sleeper?"

"The winter — ah, what fun it all was!" answered Theolette. "I wonder if I shall ever see it again."

"You shall see it every year if you will only consent to be Princess of the North," replied Florimond, with a gallant smile. And then and there the two runaways pledged their troth. The wedding over, Florimond returned to his own land, taking Theolette with him; and, unless you have heard to the contrary, they are living there happily still.

AILEEL AND AILINDA

ONCE upon a time a company of jugglers, acrobats, and other strays, traveling afoot to the Fair of the Golden Bear, arrived at twilight in a glen close by a village and encamped there for the night. From eventide till late into the dark, the watchful villagers beheld their huge fire blazing behind the dark columns of the trees; but at dawn all was still, for the wanderers had risen by the glow of the morning star, and fared away toward the sea.

Now it came to pass that an old villager, whose lands lay beyond the glen, rose early that morn, and with his hoe on his shoulder walked to his labor through the sunrise, the quiet, and the dew. Arriving at the glen, he turned aside for a moment from the path and out of curiosity wandered in to gaze at the trampled grass and the burned circle of the fire. Suddenly he caught his breath with a start. Two little children, a boy in tattered leather and a girl in a ragged frock of blue, were lying fast asleep on a pile of yellow straw.

And now the two children stood, hand in hand, in the house of the Master Villager, gazing up into the faces of a dozen gathered there to see them and to question. The little boy, who was brown-haired and brown-eyed, bore himself bravely and appeared sturdy and strong, whilst the tiny girl, whose blue eyes were full of frightened tears, seemed very gentle and shy. Of who their parents were, and of how it had fortuned that they had been thus forsaken, neither the little boy nor the girl could tell; indeed the most that could be gathered from them was that they were not brother and sister, and that the lad's name was Aileel and the girl's, Ailinda.

Forlorn, forsaken, and unknown, the children of the wanderers remained in the village and were given to certain villagers to house and to keep. It was the lot of Aileel to become the foster son and little apprentice of Braulio, the good smith, whilst tiny Ailinda fell into the hands of Tharbis, the grudging and envious miser of the town.

And now passed many years; and Aileel, of whom you first must hear, grew to be a comely young smith, wise in the lore of iron and of fire. Tall was he, broad-shouldered and very strong, yet so lithe and swift-moving withal that none in his wide land of the Blue Hills could master him in a trial of strength or speed. His favorite pastime was country wrestling, and on holiday morns you were sure to see him and his good foster father wandering down the village lanes to the day's wrestling-match, each tricked out in his best, each with a fine blue kerchief knotted at the throat. And when Aileel, after a stirring battle of catch and turn and tug and strain would hold his rival's shoulders to the straw and then leap up, light as air, joyful and victorious, how honest Braulio would shout and pound together his huge hands!

Their smithy stood by the village brook; of gray-green stone its walls were made, and its roof of heart-of-oak turned silvery brown. It was a brave sight, I can tell you, to see the fire rising hot and violet-white from the forge, brightening Aileel's face as he bent to it and gazed within it at the iron turning ruddy gold; and there was a brave music, too, in the clang-clanging of the anvil 'neath his blows.

Far otherwise, alas, were the fortunes of Ailinda! Scolded to work at the earliest dawn and kept at some task till well into the night, the poor maiden had hardly a moment's time to call her own. Whenever he could and as often, Aileel came to help her with her toil; he drew water from the well, carried in the wood, and aided her in the garden in the cool of the golden day.

In spite of this hard life, I am glad to tell you, Ailinda grew up to be as fine a lass as Aileel a lad. Her eyes were as blue as the waters of the bright September sea, the glance they gave was full of patience and courage, her long golden hair was as splendid as a queen's. Everybody loved her and helped her — all save Tharbis's only son, her jealous foster-brother, Potpan.

Squat, round-nosed, and leering-eyed, there was no spiteful trick in all the world which this wretch was not prepared to try. He would slyly nip the buds from flowers Ailinda had planted, so that they might not bloom; he would drive the cows at twilight back into the fields; he would roll the clean milk-pans in the mire. Left to his own counsel, Aileel would soon have taught the wretch a lasting lesson, but as Ailinda feared lest after such a battle Aileel be forbidden the house, she endured much, saying naught.

But presently came matters to a head.

Now it changed upon a May Day, that a fair blue kerchief had been chosen as the wrestler's prize, and this prize Aileel won gallantly, and offered to Ailinda. Gathering the kerchief together again in the folds in which it had already lain, the maiden, for fear of Potpan, hid the kerchief in a cranny of a room. Presently arrived the sunny morn of the year's midsummer holiday. At high noon, her thankless toil for a moment o'er, Ailinda went to take the kerchief from its nook.

The kerchief was no longer there!

Suddenly she heard a loud ill-natured guffaw, and turning, found Potpan at a window, watching all. He was dressed in his best festival finery, and Ailinda's pretty kerchief was knotted at his neck. The maiden's heart sank; her brave eyes filled with tears, yet she ran forth and confronted the robber face to face.

"Give me my kerchief, Potpan," said she, "Oh, give me my kerchief, Potpan!"

"Your kerchief?" answered Potpan with another rude guffaw. "Ha! Ha! That 's a good one! Your kerchief, indeed! I found this kerchief myself, and I mean to keep it, too."

"It is mine, Potpan," replied poor Ailinda. "Give me my kerchief, Potpan."

"I suppose you would wear it at the festival," jeered Potpan. "The notion of your going to the festival! Go back to your kettles and pails!"

A pause of quiet now followed, and all at once Ailinda heard through the stillness the sound of a closing gate. Suddenly Aileel came striding swiftly to her side.

"Come, Potpan," said Aileel sternly, "Give Ailinda my kerchief!"

"At your command, you wanderers' brat?" cried Potpan, furious with rage. "Be off or I 'll teach you how I — " but here his speech came to an end; Aileel, turning swiftly as the wind, caught him in a wrestler's grasp, held him fast, and undid the kerchief from his neck. This done, the young smith freed him and pushed him contemptuously aside. Hardly had he done this, however, when Potpan caught up a great stone and flung it, striking Aileel with it upon the hand.

And now there came a real tussle, for Potpan,

though squat, was no mean antagonist. A real tussle it was, but a short one, for suddenly Aileel's handsome face cleared, he laughed a little merry laugh even, and catching up Potpan in all his finery, held him high for all his kicking, walked with him a little space, and tossed him splash into the duck pond! You should have heard the squawking and the quacking of the ducks, and seen the scrambling, and the paddling, and the indignant tail-feather-shaking as Potpan fell into the mud-brown pool. One yellow duckling with cold wet feet walked on his ear.

But what an uproar awaited Aileel and Ailinda on their return from the festival!

Telling a wicked and lying story, Tharbis and Potpan had gone about among the villagers, picturing Aileel as a violent and dangerous ruffian whom it was unsafe to have about, and urging that the wanderers' lad be sent away from the village. Now Tharbis was very rich, and there were many in his debt who dared not disagree with him; a dispute arose, the village took sides, and the partisans of Tharbis and Potpan snatched the victory. At the head of a crew of hangers-on armed with sticks and scythes, Tharbis and Potpan came in triumph to the smithy, held Braulio and his foster son to the wall, and bade the latter leave the village at once, never to return.

"I go, Potpan," replied Aileel, the same strange little smile on his lips, "but I shall return some day, and I shall toss you into the duck pond once again."

"Enough! Be off, wanderers' brat!" cried Potpan's crew. "Begone, and never let us see your face again!"

So now Aileel bade his dear foster-father farewell, entrusted Ailinda to his care, and fared over hill, over dale, to the Kingdom of Iron in the Land of the Fiery Mountains.

When Aileel arrived there, it was twilight; the east behind him was already dark and blossoming with stars, and the immense plain at his feet lay full of earthy vapor and vague gloom. Night was gathering behind, night was gathering below, but beyond the vast sweep of dark the western sky was still aglow with a great splendor of the purest emerald-green. Rising steep and solitary, each one, from the dark of the plain, a thousand black mountains towered to the green light, their heads crowned with rosy glows of fire. Some from their burning craters tossed great showers of golden sparks; some were crowned with huge tongues of many-colored flames; some poured forth rolling smoke; and over others hung clouds illumined with the red of fire deep below. Presently the green of the sky deepened and died, and night came to the Land of Fire.

These Fiery Mountains, I must tell you, were the forges of the people of the kingdom, who were sturdy smiths, armorers, and artificers, one and all. Their royal city stood half upon the plain, half upon the slope of the greatest of the burning heights, and everything within it was of iron made. Of iron were the king's palace and his throne, of iron the royal crown, of iron the money, of iron the houses, of iron the walls and towers, and of iron the motionless and shrill-tongued trees along the way.

And now Aileel took service with the Lord of the Royal Forge that he might learn from him all the world's wisdom of iron and of fire. The great iron halls of the royal forge were built in the caves of the Fiery Mountains, and within them toiled Aileel from daylight to the dark, his ears half deafened with the music of a thousand anvils, and the rumbling-grumbling of the great forge-fire. Presently the Lord of the Forge became so pleased with the skill, the industry, and the good spirit of the comely young smith, that he took him to lodge in his huge iron house.

One morn Aileel said to his friend and master, "Honored sir, it is in my mind to fashion something never yet seen in the Kingdom of Iron. Grant me, I pray, the great chamber beyond the black cave to be my very own."

"It shall be yours, worthy Aileel," replied the Lord of the Royal Forge. "Here is the key."

From morn till night, behind the locked door, the people of the royal forge heard Aileel toiling at his secret task. Now they heard him at his anvil, now they heard him carrying his iron to melt in the fires of the mountain, now they heard him whistling snatches of a tune.

"What can he be making?" said they, and they peeked through the keyhole, but could see nothing at all.

But now you must hear of Potpan and Ailinda.

At first, with Aileel driven from the village and venturing afar, the poor maiden had gone about in deadly fear of Potpan and Tharbis; but as both of them had a wholesome respect for Braulio, it had fortuned that her lot was neither worse nor better than before. Tharbis still scolded her to work, shirking Potpan gave her oft a heavy task, yet day by day, in spite of all their ugly tricks, brave and patient Ailinda grew to be quite the loveliest maid in all the land. Finally even Potpan himself began to see her loveliness, and told her one evening that they were to be married in a fortnight's time! Wild with anxiety and determined to run away rather than enter into any such hateful alliance, Ailinda sought out Braulio and told him of her plight.

"Fear not, Ailinda," said the brave smith. "Though a fortnight be but a little time, and the Kingdom of Iron a week's journey down the world, yet shall Aileel be here before this wedding comes to pass. I will fetch him myself and at once!"

And now Braulio climbed to the saddle of his huge white horse, and galloped off on the road to the Fiery Mountains. Alas, just as the smith was descending the slope to a glass bridge over a river, the white horse stumbled and fell, throwing Braulio over his head and laming him severely. Hobbling along, lame horse, lame master, the pair made so slow an advance to the Kingdom of Iron, that it was not until midnight of the thirteenth day that Braulio knocked at the iron door of the Lord of the Royal Forge.

Seated in a great chair of wrought black iron, Braulio poured forth his unhappy story to Aileel, the Lord of the Royal Forge, and the latter's good wife. Strange to say, an odd little smile gathered on Aileel's lips as he heard the tale, even such a smile as he had worn when he had tossed Potpan in the pool.

"The wedding morn of Potpan and Ailinda?" said Aileel. "That shall never be! Come, take heart, good friends, and quick, all of us to the chamber in the cave!"

The night was clear and windless, but only the brightest stars were to be seen, for the great Fire Mountain above the city was crowned with an immense whirl of gold and orange flame which flooded town and sky with flaring light. Up a broad iron stair, along the slope, and into the mountain through a mighty iron portal, fled the little company. Bright torches gleamed in the iron halls and caves, the roar of the great forge shook the earth, and the iron floors were warm beneath their feet. And now as Aileel unlocked his door and flung it open wide, his friends uttered together a great cry of joy and surprise.

The young smith had fashioned a wonderful flying bird of iron! Its wings, which it flapped like a real bird, were of iron tempered a lovely jewel-blue, its breast was of iron forged to a silver-gray, and its beak and claws and living round eyes were of iron as red as fire. Within it a spring of iron lay, which one wound up with a huge black key; one steered it by pulling shiny iron chains attached to a collar round its neck. And there was a great comfortable seat, too, in the body between the wings — a seat with a huge high back in the fashion of a splendid sleigh, cushions of sunniest larkspur-blue, and just enough room for three.

So Aileel wound up the spring, clickety clack, clickety clack, clickety clack, bundled Braulio into the seat, swung back a lofty door he had opened in the side of the mountain, waved farewell, and flew out into the golden glow of the fiery night. Over the forges of iron he fled, and saw their flaming deeps and felt their hot breath; he winged his way over woodlands and mountains and rivers and gleaming lakes. Braulio, beside him, hung on to his hat all the time, and only once in a while looked over the side. On and on went Aileel and Braulio, yet the sunrise found them far away from the land of the Blue Hills.

And now it was the wedding morn and the wedding hour; the sun was shining, bells were ringing, and music was sounding in the street. Fearful of her running away, Potpan had locked Ailinda in her chamber, first advising her to put on a merry countenance lest she be well slapped. Presently women of the village came to attire her in wedding finery, and Ailinda, her heart sunken in a despairing dream, suffered them to do their will.

The bells were ringing now their loudest peals, and presently Potpan pushed Ailinda rudely up to a place on the seat of the gay cart which was to carry them to the wedding festival. This bridal cart was painted a fine bright blue, its sides and the spokes of its two great wheels were garlanded with flowers, an arch of flowers had been built over the seat, and the two snow-white oxen who drew it brandished horns gilded with bright gold.

Clang! clang! ding dong dong! went the village bells. Swaying their huge heads from side to side, and ringing golden bells upon their yoke, the white oxen slowly drew Potpan and Ailinda down the village street.

And now all at once there were cries and shouts of alarm. "Run! run, everybody! Run! Run! The bird! Oh, see the bird!" Soon one and all were scrambling here and there into houses, down cellars, under tables, into clothes-closets and up trees till there was not a soul in sight. Never stopping to take thought of Ailinda, cowardly Potpan leaped from his seat at her side, and ran and hid in a plum tree.

All, all alone stood the gay cart in the deserted street, all, all alone sat the deserted bride. The oxen came to a halt. A bell somewhere on their harness jangled, and then the world was very still.

Nearer and nearer and lower and lower through the sky came the giant bird, flapping its shining wings. Suddenly its shadow fell across the cart. Ailinda sank in a swoon against the arch of flowers. But now the great bird settled to earth on its claws of red iron, and tall Aileel, leaping forth, gathered Ailinda in his strong arms, and waked her from her sleep. Closed now were the gates of unhappiness; open were the gates of joy.

"Where is Potpan?" said Aileel sternly. Ailinda, recovering from her swoon, made faint

And now, all at once, there were cries and shouts of alarm. "Run! Run, everybody! The bird! Oh, see the bird!"

motions in the direction of the plum tree.

And now Aileel disappeared for a little while, and all at once there was a yell, a terrible splash, and a loud chorus of the most indignant squawking and quacking. Aileel had tossed Potpan once more into the duck pond!

Then Aileel came back, tall and handsome as could be, and lifted pretty Ailinda to the seat in the iron bird. Then he got in himself, set the wings to flapping, and guided the iron bird into the air and home to the wonderful Kingdom of Iron.

And there, in the house of the Lord of the Royal Forge and amid great rejoicing, Aileel and Ailinda were wed. Good Braulio, I am glad to say, remained with them, and all three lived happily together all their days.

THE WONDERFUL TUNE

ONCE upon a time, a young minstrel wandered over hill, over dale, through the world, earning his bread as he strayed by piping on a penny-pipe to all who cared for a tune. Young was he and little of stature, his eyes and his hair were brown, and in bright blue was he clad.

Now it came to pass that, as he wandered through the world, the little minstrel said to himself one morn, "If some tunes make people merry, and others make them sad, whilst still others make them dance, why should there not be a tune so wondrously pleasant and gay that all who chance to hear it must remain joyous of heart, and can never be sad or bad or unhappy again? Down the roads of the world I shall seek the wonderful tune."

And, with this new thought in his mind, the little minstrel continued on his way through the world, bidding good-morrow to all, questioning all. And some there were who thought him mad and were scarcely civil; others pushed him aside as a jesting vagabond; and there were even those who would have cast him into prison as a disturber of the public mind and a wandering rogue. But there were others, too, and these were the brave and the merciful and the kind and the merry, who speeded him on his way and wished him luck in his quest.

The summer ripened and came to an end; the crackled leaves tumbled and fled before a howling wind; snow covered the lonely fields; and still the little minstrel roamed the world, seeking the wonderful tune.

Now it fortuned that, as the little minstrel turned his steps to the west, he arrived in the city of a king whose court musician was said to know all the tunes in the world. Travel-worn, brown of face, and humbly clad as he was, the youth made his way through the palace and, cap in hand, knocked gently at the great musician's door.

From behind the little green door, long runs and wiggles and cascades of tinkling notes came dancing out into the quiet of the deserted marble corridor. The youth knocked yet again. Presently the notes ceased, and, opening the door with a stately bow, the court musician invited the young wanderer within.

And now the youth found himself in a pleasant room, painted a fair apple-green and set about with panels edged with gold; the furniture, too, was painted green and gold, and there were flowered curtains, a dozing cat, and a china bowl. As for the court musician, he was clad in a superb costume of the most fashionable lavender brocade.

"Honored Master," said the little minstrel respectfully, "I am roaming the world for a tune so pleasant and merry that, once men have heard it, they can never be sad or bad or unhappy again. Pray do you know this wonderful tune?"

"Yes, indeed, I know many a wonderful tune,"

replied the court musician. "Listen, now, was it this?" And, seating himself at a gay green-and-gold harpsichord, the court musician played a merry song full of the most elegant tinkles and trills.

"No, I am sure that is not the wonderful tune," said the little minstrel, looking through an open window at tiny clouds sailing the sunny sky of a mild midwinter day.

"Then surely this is it," said the court musician, playing a second merry tune.

But the little minstrel shook his head once more.

"Dear me, dear me! Not the wonderful tune?" exclaimed the court musician, wrinkling his brow and pursing his lips. "Ah! Wait! I think I have it!" And this time he lifted the cover of the green-and-gold harpsichord so that the minstrel could see the little picture of frolicking shepherds painted upon it, and played a long, harmonious, and majestical strain.

But the little minstrel shook his head again.

"My young friend," said the court musician, with something of a fatherly air, closing the harpsichord as he spoke, "I have played for you the only three tunes I know which might be the wonderful tune. Are you quite sure you are not wasting your life upon this quest? Perhaps such a tune as you tell of was once known in the world, and is only hidden away; yet again, perhaps it is all only a dream. You should go to the Kingdom of Music, and inquire."

"The Kingdom of Music," cried the youth. "I 've never heard of such a realm. Pray, sir, by what road does one go?"

"Come!" said the court musician, taking the youth by the arm and leading him to the open window. "See you that land of blue cloud-capped hills at the world's edge, and the broad and winding river which disappears among them? You have but to follow that stream. Farewell, young friend, the world is before you, and may you find the wonderful tune!"

League after league and day after day, the little minstrel followed the winding river, till spring stood upon the hills. And now, with the first sight of the new leaves, the little minstrel arrived in the land of melody. It was a goodly land, this Kingdom of Music — a rolling land of great fields, sweeping cloud-shadows, and ancient oaken groves: a land of pleasant murmurs and sweet sounds. Only birds with pretty songs dwelt in the Kingdom of Music, and they sang more sweetly there than in any other kingdom of the world; the very crickets had a more tuneful chirp, the river a more various music, and even the winds blew merry tunes as they whistled through the trees.

Rejoicing in the kingdom and its sounds, the little minstrel was strolling along, half in a dream, when of a sudden sky and land were filled with a strange, huge, earth-shaking sound, a sound of the scraping of thousands of fiddles; of the blowing of thousands of horns, flutes, trumpets, trombones, and clarinets; of the clashing and clanging and thumping and bethumping of thousands of bass drums, kettledrums, and cymbals; indeed, in all his wanderings the little minstrel had never heard such a din.

The King of the Kingdom of Music was rehearsing his orchestra.

Every single person in the kingdom, whether man, woman, or child, was a member of this orchestra. Babies alone were excepted, though on one occasion the King had made use of a gifted child with a musical howl!

Now, when the rehearsal had come to an end and quiet had returned to the land, the little minstrel made his way to the royal city, obtained an audience with the King, and asked for news of the wonderful tune.

"The wonderful tune," said the King from his throne, nodding gravely. "Yes, once there was even such a wonderful tune! In those days peace and plenty reigned in the world, and everyone was happy at his task beneath the sun. One luckless eve, alas! the tune in some manner happened to get broken up into notes; and before anyone could help it, these notes were scattered and lost through all the kingdoms of the world. Young man, I fear your search is in vain; never more shall the sons and daughters of men hear the wonderful tune."

"But perhaps someone might gather the notes together again," said the little minstrel eagerly.

"Many have tried to do so," replied the King. "Of those who fared away, some returned weary in the days of their youth, others crept back in old age, and others yet were lost forevermore. And never a one returned with a single note of the wonderful tune."

"Then is the time come for a new search," cried out the little minstrel bravely. "Farewell, O King of the Kingdom of Music, for I must be off gathering the notes in the highways of the world."

"Farewell, good youth," answered the King.

"Return to us when your quest is ended; and may you come piping the wonderful tune."

And now the little minstrel found himself on the roads of the world again, strolling from the first chill gold-and-gray of laggard dawns to the twilight world of meadows in the gathering dark and village bells sounding faintly afar.

Seven long years rolled over the world; the little minstrel searched diligently and far and wide, yet never a trace could he find of a single note of the wonderful tune. His blue coat, which had been so gay, was now sadly tattered and torn; even his penny-pipe had a dent in it, and his shoes, alas! were scarce worth the putting-on in the morn.

Now it came to pass, on a day in the early winter, that the little minstrel arrived in a northern land and followed a woodland road through the silence and the cold. The sky was overcast with a wide tent of dull gray cloud, through which a sun swam, cold as a moon; and the whole world was very still — so still indeed that the only sound the little minstrel could hear was the scattering of the leaves beneath his feet. Twilight came, and found the little minstrel far from a house or village; a cold wind arose, and presently a thick snow began to fall. And now the night and the snow closed in upon the wanderer. Huddled in his ragged cloak, the little minstrel trudged bravely on into the whirling storm; but little by little the cold crept into his body and bones, a weariness and a hunger for sleep overcame him, and suddenly he sank unknowing in the brambles by the road.

When he opened his eyes again, a great open fire was burning before him on a huge hearth; a blue mug of steaming milk lay waiting at one side; and over him there bent anxiously two kindly young folk — a sturdy country-lad in a green smock, and a pretty lass in a dress of homespun brown. These twain were a young husband and wife who lived in a little house in the wood, loving each other dearly, working contentedly at their daily tasks, and dealing hospitably and generously with all. Returning through the storm from a distant sheepfold, the young countryman had found the little minstrel lying in the snow and had carried him on his shoulders to the shelter of his home.

After a few days had passed, and the little minstrel felt quite himself again, he told his generous friends of his search for the notes of the wonderful tune. It was at night that he told of his quest; the supper had been cleared away, the house was still, and the little minstrel and his hosts were gathered by the fire.

"A note of the wonderful tune — bless me, but I think we have one in this house!" exclaimed the young wife. And she went to the mantel and fished about in an ancient brown bowl standing in the gloom. "Yes, here it is, sure enough — a note of the wonderful tune!"

And thus did it come to pass that the little minstrel obtained the first note of the wonderful tune; for the young husband and wife were quick to make a gift of it to their guest. But now you must hear how he found all the notes save the last.

The second note the little minstrel discovered on a glorious midsummer day. It had lain in an old bird's-nest in the heart of a great tree, and a chance breeze tumbled nest and note together at the minstrel's feet.

The third note had been hidden away amid the books of a famous scholar who lived all alone in an ancient tower, gathering the wisdom of the world.

The fourth note was given the minstrel by a little child whose toy it was.

The fifth note was turned up out of the earth, on a spring morning, by a whistling ploughman who saw the minstrel passing by and called to him to come and see the strange thing he had found.

The sixth note the minstrel had of a weaver, who labored in his own house at his own loom and upon it wove fair and beautiful things.

The seventh note a great nobleman possessed; he dwelt in his castle free of little fears and mean rivalries; and truth and courage and honor were his squires.

The eighth note the minstrel had of a young sailor, who chanced to discover it in an old ship that sailed the seas.

Of the ninth and last note, however, there was still no sign; so the little minstrel put the eight others into his pocket that had no hole in it, and turned again to his quest. And presently he walked over a hill into the Kingdom of the Blue Lakes, where reigned the Lady Amoret.

Now the Kingdom of the Blue Lakes was quite the fairest of all the kingdoms of the world, and Amoret the fairest Queen. Her palace stood on an open hill by her kingdom's eastern bound; of golden-white marble was it made, and from its terrace one looked westward to distant mountains over a woodland bright with lakes. All day long there a gay court of lords and ladies in silks and fine array held festival; the music of lutes and violins was ever to be heard; and scarce an hour there was but had its pleasure, and scarce a pleasure but had its hour.

Clad in a queen's robe of scarlet and cloth of gold, and seated in a jeweled throne raised upon the terrace, the Lady Amoret received the ragged pilgrim of the tune.

"The last note of the wonderful tune?" said the Lady Amoret. "Seek no more; it is here. Beyond the palace domain, by a lake in the depths of the wildwood, my court fool has built for himself a bower, and upon its wall hangs the last note of the wonderful tune. Tarry with us a while, and you shall have it. I promise you."

"May I not go this very instant and find it, Your Majesty?" asked the little minstrel anxiously. "Long have I roamed the world in search of it, and I need it so for the tune!"

"Nay, tarry a while," answered the Queen, unyielding; "for even were I to bid you go, you would never find the bower, so cunningly is it hidden in the wood. You have wandered long and afar, good friend; tarry now a while from your quest. My kingdom is the fairest in the world, and you shall have all you desire."

And Amoret gave a command that new apparel of the fairest blue cloth be prepared for the little minstrel and that a place be set for him at the royal board.

Now it came to pass that, as the Lady Amoret and her court beheld how brave a youth the little minstrel appeared in his new apparel, and hearkened to the thousand wonderful tales he had to tell of his quest, they found him the best company in the world and determined to hold him in the realm. To this end, therefore, they strove to drown the memory of his quest in a tide of gayest merriments; but, in spite of feasts and festivals, the little minstrel never once forgot the last note of the wonderful tune.

Try as he might, the little minstrel could never find the note. Again and again he had tried to make his way to the fool's bower, only to lose himself in the tangled paths of the wild-wood; again and again he had questioned the court fool, only to be met with a mocking courtesy, a finger to the lips, and a jesting wink of the eye. One day he even ventured to remind the Lady Amoret of her promise, but she only laughed at him for his impatience and swept him off in her golden boat to a pageant on the lakes.

Now it happened on the following morning that the Lady Amoret, taking counsel with her court, determined to destroy the note, lest the minstrel should discover it, and go. Summoning the captain of the palace guard before her, she said to him: —

"Go to-night to the bower of the court fool; take the last note of the wonderful tune, and fling it into the depths of the lake."

And now it was night, and the lords and ladies of the court, strolling forth from dinner, walked through the palace to the terrace of the west. A storm was gathering afar, an approaching thunder growled, and lightning, flashing in the sky, was mirrored in the waters of the lakes. Presently there came wind and a patter of rain, and soldiers of the palace guard entered to close the windows and the doors.

The little minstrel stood apart by a great window, gazing forth into the darkness and the storm. His fine new clothes weighed like lead upon his shoulders; his jeweled neckcloth scarce left him free to breathe; and with all his heart he longed for his rags, his liberty, and the cool rain on his eyes.

But the last note — he could not leave that behind. Suddenly he heard one soldier say to another: —

"Our companions will be caught in the storm; they have ridden forth with the captain to the fool's bower, to destroy the last note of the wonderful tune."

"Oh, the note, the note, my note! Oh, what

shall I do?" cried the minstrel, his heart sinking into depths of despair. "Even now it may be lost to the world — this time forever! I must find the court fool; he shall tell me where the bower lies!" And he looked about in the splendid throng for the fantastic motley of the fool; but he saw only many in rich garments, and the gleam of jewels reflecting many lights.

Suddenly he chanced to recall that the court fool dwelt in the garret of the palace, so up great and little stairs he fled to the fool's chamber in the eaves. The rain was now falling in torrents on the roof close overhead, and all at once a terrible peal of thunder shook the palace to its depths. Never pausing to knock, the little minstrel burst in at the door.

Candles were burning within the humble chamber, lightning flared at an oval window, and the court fool stood in the centre of the floor, still in his motley clad.

"My friend," said the court fool, with a low bow and a mocking smile, "allow me to present you with the last note of the wonderful tune." And with those words he handed the note to the very much astonished youth.

"I feared lest mishap destroy it," continued the court fool, "so yestereve I took it from my bower. You see, I believe in the wonderful tune; and without my note, this last note, your tune would scarce be worth the playing. And now, your hand, little minstrel, for you must hurry away at once through the wind and rain."

So the minstrel pressed the hand of the court fool and, hastening down a tiny corner staircase, went forth into the storm. And as he fled, he cried aloud to the thunder and the rain and the wild wind: —

"The wonderful tune, the wonderful tune! I have it, I have it — the wonderful tune!"

And now the storm wore itself away, the summer stars shone forth in the clearest of blue skies, and the only sound to be heard was the rain drip-dripping from the trees. Drenched to the skin, but with a fire of joy in his heart, the minstrel hurried through the night toward the Kingdom of Music far away.

When he arrived there, on a summer's morning, he found the people of the palace assembled in the hall of state, and the King upon his throne.

"I have it, Your Majesty!" cried out the little minstrel breathlessly; "I have it, every note; here is the wonderful tune!"

"What! The wonderful tune?" cried the King, leaping to his feet. "Quick, somebody, ring all the bells, send trumpeters through the streets, assemble the orchestra, and call hither the Violinist-in-Chief, the Lord Organist, and the Grand Harper. We shall play it over at once!"

"H-m," said the Violinist-in-Chief, after he had put on his huge spectacles and studied the wonderful tune, "Don't you feel that those last bars ought to be played very fast, like this: tum-diddy-tum — tum-diddy-tum — tum-diddy-tum — diddy-dum-dum-dum?"

"No, I do not agree with you," shouted the Lord Organist

"No, I do *not* agree with you," replied the Lord Organist, a huge personage with a majestic air and a bad temper. "Those bars should be played slowly," here he waved a large, solemn finger, "like this: tum — tum — tum — tum — tum — tum — tum — tum — tum!"

"You are both entirely wrong," interrupted the Grand Harper, a short contradictory fellow with long arms and long fingers. "To my way of thinking the entire tune should be played throughout in the same time, in this fashion; listen to my tapping now: da-da — dee-dee — da-da — dee-dee — da-da — dee-do-dum."

"Impossible! Absurd! No, never!" cried the Lord Organist and the Violinist-in-Chief in one long indignant breath. "We appeal to the King!"

But the King had ideas of his own on the matter.

And thus it was that the musicians all took to quarreling as to how the wonderful tune should be played, and are quarreling still.

But some day they will make up their minds as to how it should go; the little minstrel will leave the Kingdom of Music and come through the world piping the tune; and then, oh, then, what times there will be!

THE MAN OF THE WILDWOOD

ONCE upon a time, on a summer's morning after a night's rain, a country squire's son stood within an arched doorway of his father's house, gazing upon the hedgerows and the fields. The sun was shining after the storm, a high wind was shaking the trees, scurrying gusts fled through the nodding grass, and silvery white clouds sailed the arching sky. And beholding the bright morning and the rain-washed land, a great longing came into the heart of the squire's son to follow the clouds over hill, over dale, and to see the world. Presently, with his parents' blessing locked in his heart's treasury and a purse of gold in his pocket, he leaped to the saddle of his dappled steed, waved his plumed hat, and galloped away.

Long he rode and afar, and presently he found himself in the heart of the deepest and darkest wildwood that was ever to be seen. Before him, behind him, around him all about, were the trunks of numberless trees — trees so tall that they hid the sky, and made of it but patches of cloudy white or speckles of blue; trees — broad trees, slender trees, trees that were like men-at-arms, trees that were shy and aloof as maids, trees that were silent, trees that rustled, everywhere trees. And deep was the wildwood silence and unbroken save for the soft pad of the horse's hoofs and the rare song of a hidden bird.

At the close of his third day, the squire's son found himself at the gates of a noble city built of cedar-green glass on an open hill in the heart of the wildwood.

Now as it was late in the day when the youth arrived at the city, it came to pass that he went to an inn for supper and the night. The mistress of the tavern, I must tell you, was a lonely orphan maiden named Miranda. Surely there was never a fairer or a kinder little maid!

Beneath her ancient roof the humble wayfarer met with as friendly a greeting as his richer fellow, and with her own hands she gave bread and milk to the unfortunate and poor.

Now it chanced that the youth had been given a chamber overlooking the court of the inn, and presently he heard from below a confused din of voices, laughter, and jeers. In wonder as to what the cause of the hubbub might be, the squire's son drew open his latticed window and looked down. A great green cage on wheels was to be seen there, surrounded by a throng of curious onlookers who poked fingers at something within it, shrieked catcalls, whistled, and laughed to split their sides.

The youth descended to the court, and made his way into the throng.

Within the cage, clad in a gray wolf's skin, sat a creature like unto a man. Strong of body was he, and beautiful to behold. His eyes were blue and they were the eyes of a wild thing, and the long hair which fell about his neck was of the strangest tawny gold. Aware of the stir made by a newcomer, the prisoner turned, and fixed the youth with a glance in which lay pride mingled with despair.

Presently the proprietor of the cage, who had been baiting his horse at the stables of the inn, returned and lowered curtains about the cage and the prisoner. Fearful lest they be summoned to pay the showman his penny, the onlookers took to their heels, and soon the youth found himself alone in the courtyard.

Now this prisoner, I must tell you, was known as the Man of the Wildwood, for some hunters had found him in a net which they had spread in the wildwood a year before. To some an animal-like man, to others a man-like animal, the Man of the Wildwood remained a mystery in the land. As for the prisoner, never a word said he, and none knew whether he would not or could not talk.

Securely locked in his cage, the Man of the Wildwood was shown to all at a penny a head.

And now, as the youth mused alone in the silence, the maid Miranda came forth to light the great lantern in the court. A white apron she wore, a great white cap, and there were red ribbons on her gown. The squire's son thought he never beheld a maid so fair.

Catching sight of the squire's son, standing idly by, Miranda said to him, "Pray, good sir, what may there be in yon cage?"

"The Man of the Wildwood," replied the youth. And he told Miranda what he had overheard amid the throng.

"Alas, poor creature," said the gentle maiden, "how bitter must be such a cage to one who has known the freedom of the wildwood! I surely must bring him some honey and bread!"

And away she sped to the larder of the inn to fetch the good cheer. The twilight deepened. When Miranda returned again, the youth and the maid walked to the green cage and offered the gift to the Man of the Wildwood.

For a little space the prisoner, crouched in a

dark corner of the cage, made neither sign nor sound. Then slowly, very slowly, he approached the gift of the kind maiden and ate of it hungrily. And because he had met with so little pity and compassion, the Man of the Wildwood was moved to his heart's deep, and gazed upon the young folk with strange eyes.

All evening long the squire's son mused on the Man of the Wildwood. Suddenly a great pity possessed him, and going to the showman, he purchased the prisoner for fifty golden crowns.

And now it was midnight; and the green cage, drawn by the showman's horse, rolled down a deserted road to the edge of the wildwood. A moon almost at the full sailed the high heavens, now vanishing under thin, black clouds, now floating forth through silvery rifts and isles. Side by side, saying little to each other, sat the showman and the youth.

Suddenly a high wall of rustling darkness loomed before them at the verge of a moonlit field; the cage had reached the gate of the forest. With a key given him by the showman — who was a little afraid — the squire's son unlocked the cage, and freed the Man of the Wildwood. And even as he did so, a summer breeze went singing through the wildwood with a great cry of joy.

Free at last, the Man of the Wildwood said naught, but lifted his head to the stars. Then raising his right arm high above his head, he made a stately sign of salutation to the youth, and walked like a king into the darkness of the trees.

The next morning the youth rose early and set forth once more upon his travels. Cities he saw, and nations, and kingdoms, but no one in them whom he thought fairer than Miranda. As for Miranda, scarce had the squire's son ridden away, than she began to hope for his return.

Little by little the tide of summer rose to its full, and ebbing, left the gifts of golden autumn in the fields.

But now you must hear of the three merchants, the moonstone, and the misfortunes of Miranda.

It was a harvest eve, and presently Miranda, watching by the tavern door, beheld three men habited as merchants making their way along the city street to the inn. Somewhat to her surprise, they came afoot. Two of these merchants, I must tell you, were tall and lean, whilst the third was short and fat and had green eyes. Unwilling to refuse, yet somewhat against her better judgment, Miranda granted the request of these merchants for lodgment at the inn.

Now these three merchants, alas, were not merchants at all but three famous thieves, who had come to the city to steal a certain celebrated gem belonging to the king. This gem was a moonstone — a moonstone of such rare loveliness that men fabled that it had tumbled to earth from the moon, and been found in a forest glade at the end of a ray of summer moonshine. In all the world nothing there was more fair.

And now it was another midnight, and the three thieves, quitting their rooms in the inn, stole as quietly as three cats down the oaken stairway to the empty street. Unknown to them, however, Miranda — wakened by their whispers — followed close behind, now retreating into shadowy doorways, now leaning against a wall lest she be seen.

Presently the rogues approached the huge darkened mass of the palace, and made their way into the grounds through the dreaming gardens. A little fountain splashed somewhere in the night. The moon had set, and a thin layer of cloud dimmed the wheeling stars.

Chuckling softly at their success in having thus far eluded the palace watch, the thieves now pressed open a little window and crawled into the tower of jewels. Hurrying as fast as ever she could, Miranda ran to wake the yeomen of the guard.

Suddenly there was a great outcry, a light appeared in a window, there were shouts and a clash of arms, and the thieves came tumbling out of the window with the moonstone and vanished, all three, into the starry dark. A moment later flaming torches moved amid the trees, a throng of men-at-arms poured into the gardens, and Miranda found herself a prisoner.

Accused of having harbored the thieves and of having had a hand in the robbery, the maiden of the inn was the next morning brought to trial. Shaken to the heart, yet protesting her innocence to the last, the poor maiden made but a confused defense, and presently was condemned to suffer the sternest judgment of the law.

When this was pronounced, however, the friends and neighbors who loved Miranda made such a tumult in the court that the judgment was altered, and Miranda was sentenced to be carried in the gaoler's cart into the very depths of the great wildwood, and there abandoned to live or perish as she might.

And now it was twilight, a golden harvest twilight; and Miranda, standing with her hands tied behind her by the wrists and her head bowed low, was drawn in a two-wheeled cart through the darkening streets of the glass city, and carried far out into the pathless regions of the wildwood. Once there, the gaoler — who pitied her — loosed her from her bonds, gave her a crust of prison bread, and drove away. Fainter and fainter grew the noise of the homeward-faring cart.

The night was moonless, the stars were bright, and a wild wind from some far waste of the world was roaring through the trees, now dying away to a faint and vagrant murmur, now rising to a great wailing rustling cry that arose and broke and ebbed like a wave of the sea. And the swaying branches tossed their clots of darkness against the stars, whilst underfoot so dark it lay that naught was to be seen.

For some moments the unhappy maiden,

trembling with dread, stood motionless in the dark of the wildwood. Strange sounds drifted to her ears — the moan of rival branches, the laughter of running water, and the far cry of some hunter of the night. Suddenly she felt herself grow icy cold, and her eyes closing, she sank to the earth and knew no more.

Meanwhile, that very eve, in the distant city, the squire's son was riding joyously to the inn. Presently he reached his long-awaited goal, and to his great surprise found the windows darkened and the doorway sealed and barred. Seeing him thus wandering about, a neighboring goodwife came forth from her dwelling, and told him, with tears in her eyes, the cruel fate of the good Miranda.

"Oh, wicked judgment!" cried the youth. "Quick — tell me whither in the wildwood have they taken her; for I must find her, come what may!"

"Alas, who can say?" replied the goodwife.

"All that I can tell thee is that the cart vanished through the eastern gate, adown the eastern way."

And now the youth cried to his dappled steed to press on as he had never done before, and galloped through the night to the wildwood. Darker it grew and darker still.

Arriving at length in a little clearing, the squire's son bade his horse stand halted, and plunged into the wildwood, loudly calling and hallooing for the lost maiden. On and on through briery thicket and stony mire he blundered forward in the gloom. Suddenly an unseen ravine opened beneath him; his feet trod forward into nothingness; his hands caught at the air; and with a cry, he fell. And now as he lay there stunned, strong arms caught him gently up and carried him away.

When he woke to life again, he found himself lying on a bed of skins piled near a fire on a cavern floor. By his side, the torment of his human prison fallen from him like an evil gar-

Before him stood the Man of the Wildwood

ment, noble and beautiful and strong, stood the Man of the Wildwood.

Lifting himself up and turning toward his rescuer, the youth poured forth his story and sought the eyes of the Man of the Wildwood for a token that he had understood. For a moment, however, the Man of the Wildwood made no sign. Then, of a sudden, with a gesture at once gentle and commanding, he touched the youth by the hand, and going to the cave mouth, opened his arms to the dark wildwood, and called upon it in its secret speech.

And he bade the things of the wild — the brethren who go afoot, the kindred of the air, and the humble folk who crawl upon the earth — to go forth through the wildwood and find the maiden and guard her well. And he called upon them, too, to follow the thieves, and make them prisoners of the wood.

And now a great murmur, even such a sound as heralds the coming of a mighty rain, swept through the wood. Forth from their dens creeping came the bears, the gray wolves, and the little foxes; the shy deer started in their glens; the birds awakened with a flutter in their nests and took wing into the starry dark; the little wood-mice came tumbling out of their warm beds; and even the spotted snakes went forth to seek. Almost in less time than it takes to tell of it, the earth and the air seemed full of the people of the wild, questing here and there in search of the maid.

There passed a little time, and suddenly a great brown owl, half blinded by the firelight, swooped down to the arch of the cave-mouth with the news that he had found the maiden asleep beneath a sheltering pine; and a moment later a nimble gray hare with upstanding ears came hopping in with the tidings that the thieves had been taken on a wildwood road.

Now this news was quite enough to cure the squire's son of his fall, so jumping to his feet, he followed the staring owl and the Man of the Wildwood to the refuge of Miranda.

You may be sure that Miranda rejoiced to see the squire's son! As for the thieves, they came upon them standing terror-stricken, huddled together in the heart of a wide circle of watching, silent, flame-eyed animals. Creepers and vines had seized upon them as they fled, and bound their arms behind with leafy fetters.

Suddenly a friendly whinny was heard, and the dappled steed, guided by a benevolent badger, came trotting through the wildwood to its master. To lift Miranda to the saddle was but a moment's task. The three thieves walking ahead, Miranda riding, and the youth and the Man of the Wildwood following behind, even thus went the little company through the forest dark to the edge of the wildwood.

Morning was at hand; only the brighter stars were left in the wide and cloudless sky; presently the dawn broke over the green horizon of the trees.

Arriving at the bound of the forest, the Man of the Wildwood lifted his arm once more in token of farewell, and with his animals clustered about him, watched his friends till they vanished down the road.

Presently the domes and towers of the city of glass rose before the little company. A swirling autumn mist lay over the fields between the wildwood and the city walls, the sky was rosy overhead, and hundreds of little bells were ringing.

Pausing at the eastern gate, the squire's son delivered the thieves to the yeomen of the guard.

On the following morning the three rogues, brought to trial, declared the innocence of Miranda, confessed their wickedness, and restored the moonstone. A stern sentence was justly theirs; but so pleased was the king at the return of his jewel that he merely condemned them to road-mending for a number of years. To Miranda the king gave a rich reward, to the squire's son, a fair house whose windows looked forth on the treetops of the wildwood.

And thus it came to pass that the squire's son married the good Miranda, and lived happily with his dear wife and little ones many a long and pleasant year.

THE MAIDEN OF THE MOUNTAIN

ONCE upon a time, in a noble realm to the west of the Golden Plain, there towered to the sky a solitary height of such majesty and grave beauty that the realm became known through the world as the Kingdom of the Mountain. Mighty, snow-capped, and serene it rose beyond the little woods and willow-bordered streams.

Now it came to pass that a king ruled in the land who had been left with two little motherless children, the Prince Ariel and the Princess Leoline. The Princess was the elder of the two and, though only three years old, considered herself quite a grown-up personage; as for the little Prince, he was but a child in arms. From a window of their chamber in a tower-top, the children were wont to look forth over the land to the mountain rising afar, now blazing white and bright in the clear midwinter air, now half concealed in summer's hazy veil.

And now, with the suddenness of a tempest shattering the quiet of the night, a wicked nobleman, Babylan by name, rose against the good King and challenged him to do battle for his throne.

Now it chanced that the wise old nurse to whom the King had entrusted the Princess Leoline had for some time feared that all was not well with her master's cause, so on the day of battle she climbed to a high tower-top to see what she could see. Already from afar, through the dull still morning, could be heard the sullen tumult of the fray. Closer and closer advancing, hour by hour louder and louder growing, the tide of battle approached the very gates of the stronghold.

Suddenly, enveloped in a cloud of dust, the first stragglers from the King's defeated army burst from a little wood and came hastening down the road toward the castle. Knowing only too well that all was lost and that the troops of Babylan would be soon battering at the gate, the good nurse caught up Leoline and hurried down the curving stair to warn the guardians of Ariel.

Neither Prince nor guardian, however, could she find. The castle was already in confusion, people were running hither and thither, an alarm bell was wildly clanging, and in the soldiers' court a runaway was gasping out his story to a handful of frightened listeners. Well aware that her first duty must be the safety of the little Princess sleeping on her shoulder, the old nurse abandoned the search for Ariel and fled from the castle with her charge. And because she had been born in a village of the mountain and knew the region to be inaccessible and wild, the brave nurse turned her steps toward the height.

All night long, down lonely lane and royal highway, by woodland path and river road the brave woman hurried through the dark war-shaken land. The voice of great waters, roaring in the night under turreted bridges, beat upon her ears as she fled; messengers galloped by, spurring fast; and here and there a signal beacon flamed afar on some high crest. But presently the swarming stars grew pale, and streaks of day appeared in the east.

Pausing at a lonely farm at the end of the lowland way, the nurse begged a crock of milk and a morsel of bread for herself and Leoline.

To the east, beyond the hills, rose the great snowy summit of the mountain, outlined against a clear green sky of dawn.

And now the pleasant fields gave way to rocky wind-swept pastures, lying at the foot of a road winding and climbing along a great ridge of the mountain to a tiny village at a valley's height. To the right of this road, towering steeps of rock soared to a wild, snow-mantled crest; to the left, the mountain side fell away, a terrible precipice, to a torrent all afoam. Up this road fled the old nurse, half carrying, half dragging the weary and bewildered Leoline.

When they arrived at the journey's end, the day was at its close, the air was hushed, and the wide chasm of the valley lay dark with mist and gloom. The sun had set upon the huddled roofs of the village; but, towering into the upper air, the ruling summit still beheld the western light and reflected a rosy splendor in its snows.

Once safe in the village, the old nurse took refuge in a cottage belonging to her sister, a widow woman who kept a flock of sheep. Fearful lest the cruel Babylan in some manner become aware of the Princess and her refuge, the good woman wisely determined to keep secret the true history of her little guest. In time even Leoline herself forgot all about the palace.

Thus did it come to pass that Leoline the Princess became Leoline the Maiden of the Mountain.

As for the Prince Ariel, his fate remained a

mystery. Some said the poor little Prince had perished in a sort of prison, some whispered that the wicked new King had caused him to be abandoned in the wildwood. But, whatever the truth may have been, no one at the palace saw him or heard from him any more.

And now passed many years. Safe within her refuge in the mountain, the Princess Leoline grew from a rosy-cheeked mountain child to a tall, blue-eyed, golden-haired shepherdess. Far and wide through the villages of the height ran tales of her stout-heartedness and great daring, her gentleness and courtesy as well. Again and again, in quest of a strayaway or seeking some rare flower of the snows, she had made her way to heights to which none had ever dared aspire. Indeed, so fearless was the royal shepherdess that presently a poor woman to whom she had brought an armful of snow violets cried out to her that she must surely be under the protection of the Giant of the Mountain!

"The Giant of the Mountain," asked Leoline, "who is he? Pray tell me, for I have never before heard of him."

And she turned her head to gaze wonderingly on the wild crest of the mountain half hidden in the morning mist.

"The Giant of the Mountain is the ruler of the height," replied the village goodwife. "At least so men say, though never in my lifetime have men beheld him. Perhaps he has hidden himself away from mortals. But long ago, Maiden Leoline, in the days of the grandsires, men who climbed beyond the torrents sometimes heard a great voice speaking solemn as thunder in the hills."

"Would that I might behold him!" cried Leoline. And with wonder in her heart she returned to the daily task of watching her sheep. Clad in a pretty dress of rustic brown and wearing a kirtle of apple green, the royal shepherdess was very fair to see.

Now it came to pass on the afternoon of that

very day that, as Leoline was driving her flock home to its fold, she heard the sound of weeping, and presently she overtook a little sister-shepherdess in tears. Catching the child to her, Leoline endeavored to comfort her and asked her why she wept.

"Alas! Maiden Leoline," replied the ragged little shepherdess, "I weep because the white lamb which my father bade me guard has strayed away and is nowhere to be found. Oh, what shall I do, what shall I do?"

And the little shepherdess wept afresh, while her halted flock lowered their silly heads and bleated mournfully.

"A white lamb?" said Leoline. "Come, take heart; he cannot be far away. We shall find him, I am sure, for the sun is still high above the west, and the day is far from spent. Do you but remain here and guard your flock and mine, while I go to search the pasture by the snows." And with these words the kind maiden turned her face to the height.

Through upland pasture and rocky dell fared Leoline, scanning the waving flower-strewn grass for the lost white lamb, and listening for a forlorn crying; but of the lamb she had neither sight nor sound. Little by little the afternoon drew to a close. Presently a chill of cold and dark crept into the air as the sun vanished behind a great mass of sombre cloud.

Finding a mountain torrent near at hand, Leoline followed the edge of the roaring stream toward the wild steeps of the mountain.

The sky was now but one vast and seemingly motionless sea of cloud. Beneath this cloudy tent, however, floating strangely and swiftly by, fled steamy wisps and fragments of shapeless mist, and ever and anon one of these fugitives enveloped Leoline in its chilly veil. Bravely making her way along a path every step more dangerous growing, the maiden at length attained the last sweep of open land. Strewn with lovely flowers was the field; and two strange crags, which Leoline had never seen before, rose from its further bound.

Now as Leoline gazed upon the two crags, the level floor of rock lifted high between them, and the pinnacled wall of cliff rising behind, she beheld that they formed together a marvelous great throne, of which the two crags were the carven arms and the cliff-wall the sculptured back — a throne for a giant being mighty as the mountain: a being whose feet were of the earth and whose body rose to the clouds and the marshaled stars. And this chair stood exalted high, strange and noble and dark, now outlined against the sullen clouds, now caught up and hidden in their depths.

Presently the unseen sun sank below the crest of the mountain and a wild dark fell. The clouds rolled about the craggy throne.

And now, of a sudden, a great roaring wind arose which swept the mountain-top with a sound of noble music; the cloud veil broke asunder and rolled away; a rich and sudden

For a long moment Leoline, awed yet unafraid, gazed at the Giant of the Mountain

light poured down upon the field; and Leoline beheld the great throne uplifted high against the sunset's flare. And within the throne, mantled in a robe that might of cloud have been spun, sat a giant being. The western light was about his head, his hands rested on the crags, and there was mystery in his eyes.

For a long moment Leoline, awed yet unafraid, gazed at the Giant of the Mountain. Then came a sound like unto a far trumpet-clang, the winds were again unleashed, the clouds once more gathered together, and throne and Giant vanished in the mountain gloom.

All at once Leoline heard a pitiful cry and, looking down, beheld the lost lamb at her feet. Whence could it have come? It was nowhere to be seen a moment before.

Lifting the lamb gently up, Leoline carried it through the twilight to the little shepherdess.

And now a year and half a year again passed, and presently disorder reigned once more within the realm. Weary of Babylan and his tyrannies, the people of the land were gathering from far and wide to drive him from his throne. Surely there was never a worse King! Did he demand gold from some unhappy village, gold would he have, or else the villagers would see their houses in flames and their lowing cattle being harried to the royal barns; his prisons were full of innocent folk whose possessions he coveted or against whom he had taken a grudge; no longer in the land was to be found that friendly spirit and good cheer which had reigned there in the time of Leoline's unhappy father. But, though the anger of Babylan was the anger of the thunderstroke, there is an end to all patience; and presently the land rose against the King.

The leader of the people in this strife was a young forester of humble birth, named Norbert. This daring youth, I must tell you, had once been imprisoned by Babylan for saving a poor family from his oppression, but had succeeded in escaping to the mountain. Courteous, generous, and brave as a lion, the young Captain was the idol of the land.

Presently the tidings of the revolt arrived at the village in the mountain, and from rocky pasture and upland field the youth of the neighborhood gathered in the village square to choose their chief. And because Leoline was so spirited and daring, they cried out that she must be their leader and that no other would they obey. Riding at the head of her band of sturdy mountaineers and clad in the armor of a young knight, even thus went the shepherdess Princess to the wars.

Little by little the army of the revolt swept towards the stronghold of Babylan, and presently encamped at the foot of a huge ridge of land no great distance from the city. And there, in the meadows below the ridge, the people slept, doubting not that the next eve would see their victorious standards in the city streets and Babylan their prisoner.

But when came the dawn they beheld the terrible black horsemen of Babylan drawn up in line along the ridge. The sky was pale behind them, they moved not, and little awakening breezes fluttered their dark bannerets. Midway in the sombre rank, mounted upon a giant charger halted a little ahead of the others, was to be seen the wicked King. All at once there were trumpet calls, some near, others afar, and with a great wild echoing cry the host of Babylan swept galloping down the slope of the ridge upon the surprised soldiery of the people.

And now all was confusion indeed! A panic was at hand. Emboldened, however, by the coolness, courage, and resource of Norbert, the army of the revolt, though taken by surprise, rallied quickly and held its ground. All day long thunder of arms resounded from the fair green fields and fruit-laden orchards. Norbert performed prodigies of valor, and Leoline was ever to be found in the thick of the fray. Now at the head of her mountaineers she brought succor to an encircled group of her comrades in the revolt, now from Babylan's own color-bearer she wrested the black standard with the scarlet eagles, now was she to be seen giving water to both wounded friend and foe. But, alas! as the day grew old and the shadows lengthened, the host of Babylan slowly gained the mastery, and by nightfall the army of the people was fleeing in disorder through the highways and the fields.

Now it came to pass that Leoline, forced at length to abandon the struggle in which she had played so brave a part, discovered Norbert lying wounded and unheeded in an orchard. Dismounting from her horse, she lifted the young leader to the saddle and, accompanied by her faithful troop, hurried through the night toward the village in the mountains.

And now it was once more dawn. Presently Leoline, Norbert, and their followers arrived at the little cottage in which Leoline's old nurse and foster mother awaited her return. It was cold, and a crackling fire was burning on the huge hearth. After placing their unhappy young leader on a little pallet, the mountaineers withdrew, leaving Leoline and her foster mother to care for him. As for poor Norbert, alas! so weak was he that he lay helpless and unknowing.

And now, of a sudden, there came a swift knocking at the door, and opening it, Leoline discovered there the little shepherdess whose white lamb she had found the year before.

"Oh, Maiden Leoline," cried out the little shepherdess, "I have come to warn you! The King has discovered this refuge and is on his way here with a troop of horsemen. They are mounting the road along the ridge; my father has seen them from the high rock. Oh, make haste and hide or you will fall into his cruel hands!"

"But our Captain; what of him?" asked Leoline. "We cannot desert him in his hour of sorrow and defeat. Quick, give me your aid, and we will hide him away in yonder pines."

But the old nurse shook her head. "Nay," she said, "stir him now, and he will never again waken into life."

"Oh, Maiden Leoline, do make haste," cried the little shepherdess, holding the door ajar.

"Nay, little sister," answered Leoline, shaking her head, "here shall I remain. Farewell, little friend; I thank thee for the warning."

Now rose the morning sun in splendor over the shoulder of the mighty mountain, rolling away the mists and revealing the dewy fields, the crags, and the eternal snows in all their bright unsullied loveliness. Leaving Norbert in the care of the old nurse, Leoline ran to the high rock.

Before and below her lay the village, then the deep gulf of the valley opening toward the distant plain. All at once the Princess beheld Babylan and his men! Up the road leading along the side of the higher crest they were mounting. Ever and anon, on lesser slopes of the winding road, they galloped their steeds.

Now crept despair into the heart of the brave Leoline even as the bitter cold of a winter's night creeps into a room when sinks the fire. And in her heart she beheld the helpless Norbert in the hands of his enemy, her people flying, pursued, to the caverns in the mountain, and her village laid low.

But of whom could she now seek aid? Along the snow-crested ridge nearer and nearer rode the wicked King.

Suddenly Leoline recalled to mind the Giant of the Mountain. Turning her face toward the mountain peak, she lifted her arms to it and cried aloud: —

"O Giant of the Mountain, O Giant of the Snows, help us in our need!"

Loud and clear rang the cry of Leoline through the mountain air and was followed by a silence. A breeze shook the branches of the dwarfed pines; a bird sang.

Then, suddenly, a far high murmur trembled to a roar, a roar loud and terrible enough to drown all the sounds of the world, and from the snow-capped ridge above the road there flowed and rolled down on Babylan and his men a mighty avalanche. Huge stones were there in it, glistening ice and snow, brown earth and uprooted pines. Sweeping over the road, the mass poured over the precipice into the valley-depth a league below.

Such was the end of the wicked Babylan.

Now it came to pass that, because his horse had gone lame, one of Babylan's men had fallen behind and, as a consequence, had escaped the avalanche. Upon this fellow the mountaineers quickly fell and were about to do him a mischief when the horseman cried: —

"Hold! Hold! I, and I alone, can tell you of the lost Prince Ariel."

Hearing these words, the mountaineers thought it wise to take their captive to Leoline. Bound securely, the horseman was thrust into a corner of the cottage and commanded to tell his story to the assembled company.

"Babylan gave me the Prince Ariel," said the man at arms, "and bade me abandon him in the wildwood. But I obeyed not his cruel word and left the child with a good forester, named Hildebrand of the Oaks."

Now, when the horseman had spoken, all present knew that, by a strange and wonderful turn of Fortune's wheel, their young leader was likewise their lawful lord and king. For Norbert the daring had passed as the son of the forester, Hildebrand of the Oaks.

And now it was the old nurse's turn to speak. Said she, "Long enough have I kept my counsel, but now that the danger which kept me silent is no more, I may tell all. Our Leoline, whom you have known as Leoline, the shepherdess, is Leoline, our Princess and own sister to Prince Ariel."

And she told them all of her flight to the mountain and of how she had saved the little Princess from the cruel Babylan. You will believe that Leoline was amazed to find herself a real Princess. But her heart was filled with joy and pride because of her brother's deeds.

Now, when Ariel's wounds had healed and his strength had returned, the people of the mountain escorted him in triumph to the royal city, and there, amid universal joy, the brave Prince claimed and received his own. The annals of Fairyland tell of no better King. I am glad to say that he richly rewarded both the man at arms and the old nurse.

As for Leoline, she took the Mountain for her kingdom and, under the protection of the Giant of the Height, dwelt there long in peace and happiness.

THE BELL OF THE EARTH AND THE BELL OF THE SEA

ONCE upon a time a brave mariner, who had sailed the blue for many years, married a captain's daughter and went to live in a pleasant inland country a long way from the sea. Now it came to pass that, as the sailor and his wife dwelt in the inland vale, a sturdy son was born to them whom they named Altair; and this little son grew to manhood with a great longing in his heart to go companying with sailors and sail upon the sea. Presently the old mariner called his son unto him and said: —

"Dear son of mine, a sailor were you born and a sailor you shall be. Go you forth to the ships, have your fill of a sailor's life, and may honor and fortune come to you upon the sea."

So now the youth Altair bade his dear parents

farewell and followed the northern highway to a certain great city by the sea. Day after day, as he walked, the soft blue skies and golden clouds of the inland country vanished behind, a brightness and a faint glow of green appeared in the arching heavens, and a cold northern wind shook each sombre northern pine. Suddenly one morn the youth heard from afar the endless thundering of breakers and, arriving on a sandy height, beheld great seas tumbling in foam and white confusion on the shore. And thus discovering the sea, something in the heart of Altair shouted and leaped for joy.

To one side and below stood the towers and masts of the city; there were sailors in her streets with brown faces, rich merchants in velvet caps and gowns, brave pilots, and adventurers, and captains coming and going to their ships.

After purchasing a stout jacket, a knitted cap, a blue sailor blouse, and a pair of trousers belling out below, Altair set down his name in the book of a great ship and sailed away upon the sea. Seven years he sailed, now through nights of whispering seas and skies of silent stars, now through storms and howling winds and waves blown white with foam. Little by little the youth's blue eyes took on the look of one who sees afar, his body grew strong, and he walked as a sailor walks, with feet apart and a roll from side to side. Seven years he sailed, and then became a captain and master of a vessel of his own.

Now it came to pass that, as the blue-eyed captain returned from a long and lonely passage to the Isles of Gold, he beheld a great multitude of ships sailing together down the sea. Across his bow they sailed, great ships stately as castles of oak, little ships that bobbed and courtesied to every wave, ships with pennons, ships with banners, ships of all rigs and colors in the world. And so great was the multitude of ships that some had already crossed the rim of the sea ahead, whilst the swaying spars of others rose faint and far behind.

In great wonderment as to what the gathering might portend, the young captain hailed a passing ship and questioned a master mariner.

"These be the ships of all the world, Sir Captain," answered the master mariner, "and we sail to the land of the King of the South, for he hath summoned us one and all. There is great news, they say, awaiting us at journey's end, but of what it may be none can tell. But come: up with your helm, Sir Captain, and follow through the sea."

Week after week, through weather fair and weather foul, Altair sailed with the ships of the world to the Kingdom of the South. All at once, one fine night between midnight and the morn, the men upon the masts of the first three ships sent back a cry of land, and presently the great blue light of the Kingdom of the South shone forth, far away and low upon the sea. At sunrise the ships of the world, following one another in line, sailed through rocky gates into the wide haven of the King.

The palace of the King was built upon a hill-top between blue mountains and the sea, it was of golden marble made, and a winding marble stair led from it to a pavilion and a landing on the bay. Rising in solitary splendor above the ancient trees of the King's garden, a great belfry-tower soared to the rosy dawn which overhung the hilltop and the town.

And now, in the hall of columns, stood gathered the captains of the ships of all the world, great captains with plumes in their velvet caps and jeweled swords at their sides, merchant captains in capes of sober blue, and humble fisher-captains with knitted caps and blouses gaily striped. Then came forth to them the King of the South, clad in a scarlet robe and a crown of yellow gold, and said to them: —

"Captains of the ships of all the world, I give you greeting. You wait to hear why I have called you from the seas. Hearken then to my word. A belfry have I built, the fairest belfry which stands beneath the sun, and I fain would lodge in it the fairest and noblest bell in all the world. Find me this bell, O captains of the ships! Go ye to all nations, and speed through all the seas.

"He who finds the bell shall be given a mighty treasure, and be crowned with glory and honor."

Thus having said, the King of the South led the captains of the ships to a great feast which he had prepared for them, and there they made merry till the closing of the day.

Now, when the sun had set and the city, the still harbor, and the ships were bathed in a gentle golden light, Altair descended the winding marble stair to the pavilion at which his ship's boat lay awaiting his return. Now it came to pass that, as the young captain approached the end of the steps, he saw standing by a marble pillar there an old bent fisher-wife with a young fisher-maiden at her side. And, because it seemed to Altair that they were fain to speak to him, yet a little afraid, the young captain paused at the pillar and asked the fisherfolk if some misfortune had come upon them.

"Good Sir Captain," replied the maid, "we are fisherfolk of the Perilous Isles who would fain return to our homes again. In the spring-tide of the year, while my mother and I were out amid the nets in our little boat, a storm arose which swept us out to sea. For two bitter days and nights we fled before the gale, but on the third morn a great ship chanced to espy us and, rescuing us from the waves, brought us to this realm. Long have we sought a way to return into our own land. You find us here because of our hope that one of the ships of the world might be sailing by the Isles. But though we have asked those who passed before, there was never a one who could help us on our way."

And the old fisher-wife shook her head slowly and sadly, whilst the maid stood still and said no more. The golden light was fading now from the city, the still harbor, and the ships. Even the belfry tower stood dark, its empty bell-chamber outlined against the sky. Presently the great blue light at the harbor mouth awoke in its stately tower, and a sudden wind brought a little sound of waves on the distant outer shore.

"Be of good cheer, I will take you to the Isles," said the young captain. And, with stately courtesy, he put the fisherfolk in the boat and went with them to his ship. Then was heard the sound of ropes and blocks and the filling of sails, and presently the ship of Altair fled away like a bird into the dark sea. Already there were lights here and there on the dark waves, the lights of ships gone seeking the marvelous bell.

At the end of a fortnight of favoring wind and fine weather, the ship of Altair arrived by the Perilous Isles. Huge and high and dark were the Isles, and weed-hung reefs encircled them and tossed fountains of spray into the air.

Off the isle of the fishers, the kings of the world

had prepared a fairway — for so mariners call a passage — through the cruel rocks, and at the entrance to this passage a warning bell sank and rose and nodded and swung in the seas.

And now the fisher-maiden and her mother bade a grateful farewell to the young captain Altair and were rowed ashore to the isle. The name of the maiden, you must know, was Thyrza. Her eyes were gray, and her hair a pretty ruddy-gold. And so fair she was and so honest and true her gaze, that Altair thought he had never seen her like in all the world.

As for Thyrza, she stood long upon the shore, watching the ship of Altair until it dwindled and disappeared at the edge of sea and sky.

North and south, through the seas of the world, went Altair in search of the bell. To great cities of golden domes he sailed and found silver bells, and brazen bells, and even bells of glass, but never a bell for the belfry tower; by lonely shores he passed and saw the far surf break in a border of white between the yellow sands and the ocean's sweeping green.

Now it fortuned that the boatswain of the vessel was an old mariner who had sailed with Altair since the days of the young captain's apprenticeship at sea. And presently this boatswain came to Altair and said to him: —

"Good master, in the isles of the east was I born, and in those isles there runs a tale that somewhere, in the great sea flowing westward down the world, lies an isle of bells. There is a city there, they say, whose citizens take such joy in the ringing of bells that they will be at it all day long; in the mountains of the isle are rare metals most fit for noble bells, and there is a King there who is the bellman of the world. It may be but an idle tale, but I tell it as 't was told to me."

"East and north and unto the south have I sought the bell in vain," said Altair. "Into the seas of the west none have ever sailed.

Come, helmsman; about, about, and follow the setting sun; we shall seek this hidden isle."

Westward into the bright waves and the great glory of the sun sailed Altair. Higher grew the waves, the sun-bright spray fell in showers about the bow, and streams of marbly foam ran hissing at each side. A thousand leagues upon a thousand leagues sailed the ship, and presently there came a windless night of swaying ropes, still waters, and the stars. And, while the ship glided ever so gently on into the night, there was heard over the sea, faint and far, a golden sound of bells.

Now uttered the sailors a cry of joy which rang to the stars and drowned the voices of the bells. And a wind arose, and the sails filled, and when it was dawn the mountain isle of bells stood before them, lonely as a ship in the wide circle of the sea.

Then to the city of bells they went, and found bells on every house and tower, and people wearing bells on the borders of their gowns. All day long great bells were ringing in their towers, chimes were pealing, and clusters of little bells replying — tiny bells that sang like children at their play.

Now it came to pass that, when the old, bearded King of the Bells heard the tale of the brave voyage of Altair, his heart warmed to the sturdy blue-eyed youth and he said to him: —

"Good Sir Captain, you shall have the bell you seek, the fairest and noblest bell in all the world. To-day shall the metal be prepared and melted in the furnace of the mountains, and to-morrow at high noon shall the metal be poured into the mould of the bell."

And now it was the high noon of the following day, and the King and his people, together with Altair and his sailors, stood beside the fiery pit in which the metal of the bell boiled in foam of green and red and eddying copper-gold. Taking a golden cup filled with earth, the King cast it into the pit, saying: —

"O bell, by this token I charge thee to remember the earth!

"The earth and her sweet sounds, the songs of birds, the rustle of leaves, the murmur of brooks, the cry of the night wind, the majesty of thunder: of these speak to the sons of men!"

And thus having spoken, the old King took a golden cup of water of the sea, and cast it also into the molten pit, saying: —

"O bell, by this token I charge thee to remember the sea!

"The sea and her voices, the roaring of the mighty waves, the thin whisperings of foam, the talk of ripples on the shore of sheltered isles, the tumult of the gale: of these speak to the sons of men!"

And they poured the fiery metal into the earthy mould and left it to grow cool. Seven days and seven nights sped by, and presently came skilful men to cut the bell from the mould, and sculptors to carve upon it flowers and trees and leaves and birds and waves and cockle shells.

And Altair thanked the old King with all his heart and, stowing the bell in the hold of his ship, sailed away eastward and southward through the sea.

Now it came to pass that, as the returning voyage drew to an end, the young captain found his ship to be almost empty of victuals and drink; so he hastened to the nearest port to see what he could buy. Now it chanced that there lay in the same port another ship which was also returning with a bell, a fine bell to be sure, but not one worthy to be named with the bell of brave Altair. The name of the captain of this other ship, you must know, was Kraken, and he was filled with curiosity to see if the bell of Altair was a better than his own.

The ship of Altair lay at a wharf, and strong brown-faced men worked in the hazy sun, rolling kegs of water to the deck and carrying bags of meal down into the hold. Presently Kraken, sitting in the stern of a red boat rowed by six of his sailors, came over to call upon Altair.

And stowing the Bell of the Earth in the hold of his ship, the young Captain sailed eastward and southward through the sea

And now Altair and Kraken stood in the dark hold of the ship, and Altair held up a great light so that Kraken might see the wonderful bell. And beholding the bell, how fair it was, Kraken said in his secret heart: —

"If the Captain Altair shall return to the land of the South with this wonderful bell, my bell will never win the treasure of the King. I must find a way to destroy this captain and his bell!"

Turning to Altair he said, "Brother Captain, when do you sail away?"

"To-morrow at high noon," replied Altair.

"At high noon?" said Kraken, his envious eyes suddenly lit with a wicked thought. "You dare then to sail at night through the reefs of the Perilous Isles?"

"My ship is fast," replied Altair, "and I shall find the floating bell of the fairway before the sun has set. Once I find it, what is there to fear? The passage which it marks is deep and wide. And the Bell has a brave clang."

And now it was the next morn, and Kraken sailed early from the port. All morning he sailed over a lonely gulf of the sea, and arrived at noon before the Perilous Isles. It was a windy day, the hazy sky was now open, now overcast, and here, there, and all about the reefs were breaking white. Gulls barked and piped, and the shaggy weed-hung sides of the nearer reefs rose and fell with the waves.

Presently Kraken caught sight of the floating bell which marked the entrance to the fairway of the Isles.

The sea-bell had been made in the fiery mountain forges of the Kingdom of Iron. Its round base was of iron, and a band of iron, chiseled about with fish and shells and flowers of the sea, encircled its tossing rim. The warning bell rose from the center of the shield, and two iron figures, one of a giant, one of a dwarf, struck it with iron hammers night and day.

And Kraken laughed and sent men to break the hammers from the hands of the iron figures so that the bell should sound no more. And this they did. But the dwarf and the giant continued to lift and lower their empty hands.

Sailing through the fairway, Kraken continued on his course to the Kingdom of the South, and was soon lost to view.

The wicked deed, however, had not passed unseen. Thyrza, the fisher-maiden, had beheld all.

The long hours of the afternoon dragged to their close. Sunset was at hand. Black clouds rose over the edge of the world, the sea darkened, and the heavy waves grew black and streaked with foam. A wind began to howl.

Suddenly Thyrza beheld the sails of a great ship fleeing before the gale. The hidden sun had almost set, and the black clouds were barred with rays as red as fire.

"'T is the ship of Altair," cried Thyrza. "The night is gathering fast, and, unless he hears the bell in the dark, Altair will be wrecked upon the reefs. I must row to the bell, if I can, and sound the warning clang."

And now the courageous maiden hastened to her little fishing boat and rowed through the dark and the gathering storm to the soundless bell. Long and hard she fought, and presently a great gust of the gale swept her down against the bell. Great waves were breaking over it in bitter spray, and it rolled and tossed and turned and plunged in the sea.

After tying her little boat to one of the figures, Thyrza took a round stone, which she used as a weight for a net, and began to sound the bell.

Nearer and nearer drew the ship of Altair. The fiery bars of the sunset faded from the clouds; the wild night closed in upon the sea.

"Ding — Dong! Ding — Dong!" went the bell. And the wind howled in the dark, and the waves thundered and broke as they fled. Suddenly Thyrza saw the lights of Altair's ship close at hand; the vessel was safely entering the passageway.

So near she passed to the bell that Thyrza could almost have touched her oaken side.

Now, when the lights of Altair's vessel had vanished in the night, Thyrza went to unloose her little boat and row ashore. Some fishers had seen her on the bell and built a great bonfire on the beach to guide her safely in. But suddenly the maid beheld the lights of a second ship, searching for the fairway and the bell.

Weak and chilled though she was, Thyrza sounded the bell till this vessel, too, had passed safely through the reefs. Much to the maiden's surprise, this second vessel came about and anchored in the little fishing-harbor of the Isles!

Guided by the light of the fire, brave Thyrza safely made her way to the shore.

As for Altair, he continued on to the Land of the South, and was given the treasure and the crown of glory and honor for bringing the fairest and noblest bell.

And the bell of the earth hung in the belfry-tower, and in the morning and the evening spoke to men of the wonder and mystery of the earth and the changing sea.

And now the brave young sailor had riches and honors like unto a king, yet was he restless at heart, for he remembered the maiden Thyrza and was fain to make her his wife. Returning again to the sea, he sought the Perilous Isles, and hurried ashore to find the gray-eyed maid.

"You seek the maiden, Thyrza?" asked the fishers. "Alas! she is gone we know not where. In the month of the low moon, two great ships passed at nightfall through the fairway of the reefs; one ship continued over the sea, and the other came to anchor in our bay. We fear that this ship was perchance a pirate ship, for she sailed away at the break of dawn, and since that hour Thyrza hath not been seen."

And the fishers told Altair of how Thyrza had saved the ships by striking upon the sea-bell; and Altair remembered the night of which they spoke, and knew that Thyrza had saved him from the reefs.

East and west and north and south, along the shores of the world went Altair in search of the maid. But never a one he found who could tell him aught of her. A long year he sailed, and presently he came to the Kingdom of the Moon.

Now it came to pass that, when he went to the palace to ask tidings of Thyrza, attendants came and led him before the Queen who ruled the land. And she was very young, and clad in a silver gown, a silver crown, and a spreading robe of blue.

Strange to say, a heavy silver veil hid her face from all.

"Sir Captain," said the Queen, when she had heard the story of Altair, "you are wasting your days in quest of the fisher-maid. She is gone; you will never see her more. Have done with this hopeless seeking, and take service in my realm. Stay, and I shall make you the kingdom's admiral."

But gallant and faithful Altair shook his head and answered, "No." And though the Queen twice and even thrice besought him to stay, he still remained faithful to his quest.

Then laughed the Queen a little merry laugh, and tossed the veil aside. And Altair beheld Thyrza on the throne!

"Dear Altair," said the Queen, "you shall hear all. My father was the King of this country and I was his only child. It fortuned that one morn we went forth in a ship, and a great storm arose which drove us from our course far out into the sea. Presently the ship struck upon the reefs of the Perilous Isles and went to pieces fast. Of all aboard, I alone was saved.

"My subjects long sought for news of the missing vessel, but in vain. Years passed, and presently a fisherman of the Kingdom of the Moon chanced to land at the Isles and heard from the fishers the story of the wreck. He returned with the tidings, and my people came in a great ship to take me to my land. We hurried away, for a dangerous wind was blowing and the captain was a stranger to the reefs. But even now there is a ship on the sea which carries tidings and gifts to the fishers of the Isles."

So now the courtiers and the attendants bowed politely and withdrew, and Altair and Thyrza walked together to a great window by the sea. And there the young sailor and the Queen who was a daughter of the sea pledged their faith to one another.

Their wedding was the most splendid wedding ever seen in all the world. Altair's good father and mother were there, Thyrza's foster mother too, and all the sailors danced hornpipes and sang old pleasant songs of the sea.

And they all lived happily ever after.

THE WOOD BEYOND THE WORLD

ONCE upon a time a young knight, named Alois, went to dwell at the court of a mighty King until his coming of age, for he was without kinsmen, and heir to great powers and possessions. A tiny round room in the castle's topmost tower was given him to be his very own; and from the curving sill of its one great window he could look down on the gardens of the palace, the woodland beyond, and see the older nobles walking two by two behind the King.

Now it came to pass, upon a summer eve, that the knight Alois beheld from his tower a lovely golden light moving about on a hillside in the wood.

"The elves must be dancing on the hill," said the young knight. "I 'll ride into the wood, and watch them from afar." And gallop-a-gallop away he rode in the dark. The night was still, the birds had gone to bed, and a young sickle-moon was sinking in the west with the old moon in her arms.

Suddenly the youth beheld the golden light approaching through the trees.

A pretty maiden in a dress of homespun green, a white apron, and a little cap was carrying a golden lantern through the wood. Her eyes were upon the ground, and every once and a while she stooped to gather a flower from the earth and thrust it into a basket by her side. Dismounting from his horse, Alois followed the maid afoot, fearful lest the snapping of a twig reveal his presence in the dark.

And now the maiden came to a little house in a moonlit forest-glade and, entering the dwelling, closed the door gently behind her. A casement window stood open to the night, the beam of the golden lantern filled the room, and presently a voice began to sing a pretty country-tune. Mingled with the lilt of the ballad was a strange sound, a purring treading sound something like the whir of a spinning wheel, but heavier and with a queer wooden click to it every tiny while.

Approaching quietly in the moonlight, Alois rose on tiptoe and gazed within the house.

A single candle in a tall candlestick was burning at each end of the mantel, candles were burning in sconces on the wall, and the golden lantern, still aglow, hung close beside the door. The maiden of the light was sitting at an oaken loom, working the treadles with her feet, and tossing the shuttle back and forth from side to side. Skeins of golden thread, and white, and rose, and mulberry, and blue lay at her fingers' ends, and on the frame of the loom stood forth the finished labor, a noble tapestry in which the maiden had cunningly woven knights and ladies, banners and tents and men at arms, and castles moated round with quiet streams.

This maid in homespun green, I must tell you,

was an orphan lass who earned her bread in the world by weaving at her loom. It was her custom to stain the weaving yarns with colors made of roots and flowers, and she had been wandering about in search of the starlight daisy when Alois had seen her lantern on the hill.

Now it came to pass that, as the youth Alois rode home in the moonlight to his tower, he could think of naught but the lovely maiden of the loom and determined to ride forth again, find her, and make her his wife. On the following morning, therefore, he rode singing down the wildwood road to the house in the glade and asked a cup of water from the maid. And so graciously and prettily did Fidella — for this was the maiden's name — offer him the cup, that Alois thought her more than ever quite the most charming person in the world.

Months passed, the youth rode every day to the little house, and presently made so bold as to ask Fidella to marry him on the morrow's morn. Little suspecting that Alois was aught but a simple squire of the court, the maiden answered with a nod, and promised to be ready to ride with him to the village on the hilltop, and there be wedded by the Master Villager.

And now it was the marriage morn; great clouds fled over the sun, chilling and quieting the world, yet every now and then breaking asunder and dappling the broad land with spots of sunshine, which gleamed for a moment and were gone. Dressed in her pretty country finery, and with a nosegay of posies at her throat, Fidella stood by her window waiting to hear the thunder of arriving hoofs and Alois' joyous hail.

But, alas! little by little the morning dragged along, the wooden clock on the mantel ticked and ticked and ticked and ticked, the clouds gathered in a gray sea over the noontide sun, yet of Alois came no sign. Early in the afternoon a gentle windless rain began to fall, and presently the flowers in the garden hung their heads in the gathering gloom, as if in sorrow to see so fair a bride forsaken and forgot.

But now you must hear of what had happened at the court.

Now, after bidding farewell to the maiden of the loom and promising to return on the following morn, Alois had gone to his tower and attired himself in the magnificent costume which court ceremonial prescribed for all who were fain to speak with the King. This habit was of richest white satin, faced with gold; a sword set with splendid sapphires was belted to its side; and a short blue-velvet cape, hanging in loose folds, was secured at the breast by a golden chain. Now, as Alois was very dark and red-cheeked, you will see that this costume was really quite becoming.

Thus arrayed, the youth went boldly to the King, and spoke freely and frankly of his love for the maid of the loom and of his purpose to be married with her on the morrow's morn.

The King, who sat on his throne clad in a great scarlet robe and wearing his crown, listened to Alois with a smile when he began, but with a frown as the tale drew to an ending.

"Youth," said the King sternly, "I have heard enough; this folly must end, and at once. Are you so far forgetful of your great inheritance that you must take a weaver's lass to be your bride? Go to your tower, and see that you ride not beyond the castle wall until I speak the word!"

"But, sir, am I not in this my own master?" cried Alois, unafraid.

"You are my ward," replied the King, with cold authority, "and I have other purposes for you. Sir Alois, go!"

"Do what you will," replied the youth; "I shall have Fidella, and no other." And holding his head high, the youth Alois quitted the audience hall, and mounted to his room.

Now when he had gone, the King, who had sat silent a moment, chin in hand, suddenly threw off his crimson robe, called for his coach, and rode through the wood to a giant tower on the brink of a wild ravine. A powerful enchanter dwelt there, whose magic aid and guileful counsel were ever at the service of the King.

And now the enchanter sat in a huge golden chair hearkening to the King. He was very old, this enchanter, and attired in a full black mantle, spangled with silver stars and golden crescent-moons; and, as he sat in his golden chair, he leaned forward and rested his two hands on a stout black cane. The high round chamber was full of a cobwebby gloom, and on shelves in the arched windows stood crystal flasks of a thousand twisted shapes and colors: deep ocean-blues, fiery scarlets, smoky purples, clear topaz yellows, and bright snake-like greens. And there was a huge black lizard with greeny-scarlet eyes, that made scaly noises as it ran about on the flagstones of the floor.

When he had heard the King's story of Alois and Fidella, the enchanter smote the floor with his black cane, rose to his feet, saying never a word, and took from a niche in the wall a jar of blackest marble, strangely veined with gold.

"You have done well to come to me," said the enchanter to the King, "for the youth is proud-spirited and will resist you to the end. 'T were wisest to bend him to your will by magic guile. Within this phial dwells the water of forgetfulness; a goblin brought it me from the depths of the underworld. To-night you must pour it forth into a golden goblet, and that goblet you must stand by the youth's place at the dinner of the court. As soon as he drinks of it, he will forget the weaver's maid forever."

And now it was evening, and the King and his guests were at dinner in the castle banquet-hall. There were candles everywhere, white tables and golden plates, and much coming and going of servants clad in green. From the royal table, raised above the others, the King watched Alois through the meal. Suddenly he smiled a grim smile; the youth had drunk the cup.

When it was late at night the King summoned Alois before him, stared into his eyes, and beheld that he had indeed forgotten all.

"My Lord Alois," said the King, "your coming-of-age approaches, and you will soon find yourself the greatest lord in my dominions. Since you are my ward, it has been my duty to seek for you a bride worthy of your titles and estate. In the Kingdom of the Fields a fair Princess dwells. Melusine is she called, and to-morrow's morn you shall go forth in state to offer her your homage and your hand."

Thus spake the crafty King, and hid in his heart his design of adding the Kingdom of the Fields to his own dominions through the marriage of the knight and Melusine.

And now it was the morn of cloud and fleeting gleams of sun. In the little house in the glade, Fidella stood waiting and waiting at the casement window; whilst at the court, Alois drew on his jeweled gloves, bowed to the King, mounted into the golden coach, and sank back in splendor against cushions of mulberry brocade.

"Tick-tock, tock-tock, tick-tock," said the clock in Fidella's house, as the hands circled the hours.

And the golden coach, gleaming great golden gleams in the pools of light, rolled over the hills and far away.

It was twilight now and, in the little house in the wood, Fidella lifted the bridal wreath from her head, lit candles, and sank into a wing chair by the burnt-out embers of the fire. So great was her trust in Alois, that never a questioning doubt of him raised its voice in her heart.

"Some evil thing has surely come to pass," said faithful Fidella. "Alas! what may it be?" And for two days she walked to and fro between the window and her loom, vainly hoping for a sign. On the third morning, no longer able to bear the burden of her fears, the maiden journeyed to court and sought news of Alois from the King.

"So you are the maid of the loom?" said the unpitying King, who owed Fidella a grudge for having endangered his precious schemes. "And 't is your Sir Alois whom you seek? Well, find him if you can. Ho, guards of the palace, take this forward maid, put her in a coach, and drive her far beyond the bounds of my dominions!"

Over hill, over dale, bumping through puddle-holes, and tossing and swaying crazily from side to side, rolled the coach in which Fidella sat a prisoner. A rushing scurrying wind was flowing over the sunny world, shaking the manes of the galloping horses, rippling the roadside pools, and worrying the little birds who had just begun to fly. Presently Fidella found herself on a lonely moor, watching the coach fare homeward into the wind-streaked splendor of the west.

And now began the wayfaring of Fidella in quest of Alois, for the King had forbidden the maid to return again into her own land. Down the highway of the Golden Plain she fared and beheld the grain tossing about her like a sea; through the silence of the Adamants she passed, and on into the Kingdom by the peaks; yet never a word of Alois brought joy to her ear.

Now it fortuned on a spring morning, as Fidella wandered in a pleasant land of wooded hills and little singing brooks, she came to the strangest palace that was ever to be seen. Of earth o'ergrown with grass were its mighty walls and lofty battlements; flowers grew in the crannies; blossoming vines swayed from its heights; and, when the maiden peered within, she beheld there a woodsy hall, whose giant columns were the trunks of living trees. At the far end of the hall, on a throne of living wood, sat a dark and stately queen. Twelve maidens stood beside her, three robed in summer scarlet, three in winter white, three in springtide emerald, and three in russet gold.

The lady of the palace was Airda, the great

Earth Queen. Four sons had she, and each son was master of a season of the year.

"My faithful Fidella," said the Earth Queen, when she had heard the maiden's story, "be of good cheer, for all that hath been hid from you shall now be known. An enchanted torrent through my palace flows; its waters possess the gift of speech, and to every mystery it hath a secret key. Follow, Fidella, to the grotto of the stream."

Now rose the Earth Queen from her throne and led the way through the cool sweet-smelling chambers of the palace to a strange dark grotto, half cave, half vine-hung hall. At the darker end of the leafy cave a lovely waterfall, whose torrent was full of a pale mysterious light, was leaping from some height overhead into a chasm so profound that only the faintest watery murmur rose in whispers from below. Kneeling upon the brink of the chasm, Fidella gazed down into the palely glowing depths of the abyss and asked of Alois and his fate.

For a moment or two, the waters far below seemed to gather themselves into a faint echoing roar, which slowly ebbed to a whisper; and presently this whisper became a voice, and dissolved into delicate and silvery words. And the voice of the enchanted chasm told Fidella of Alois' true faith, of the enchanter and the water of forgetfulness, and of the youth's journey to the court of the Kingdom of the Fields.

"Ah, me! Is there no way in which the spell may be broken?" said Fidella.

"In the wood beyond the world," answered the torrent, "under trees which are older than the stars, the fountain of memory pours its crystal stream. If the youth shall drink a golden goblet of this water, the chain of the spell will break." And the silvery voice grew faint, and died away.

And now Airda, the Earth Queen, gave the maiden a fair golden goblet with a golden cover, and bade her sail upon the giant ship of the earth to the wood beyond the world.

When the maiden arrived at the sea, the sun had vanished below mountains to the west, the waves were breaking gently along a darkening shore, and ragged hulks of cloud were lying becalmed in the deep and starry sky. Far, far out to sea, rising from the waters like the blue bulwark of another land and bridging the vast horizon from west unto the south, stood the giant ship of Airda, the Queen. So high were its masts that their tops could scarce be seen in the dome of the heavens, clouds swept through the royal yards, and the lights within the rigging floated like stars upon the sky.

Three days' journey long, and close upon a day's journey wide, was the giant ship. Its sails were the size of towns, and a sailor on horseback carried the captain's orders to the crew. And there were villages aboard, and wide fields in which men were ploughing, and grazing cattle, and highways, and inns wherein travelers might rest.

Now came the dark, a wind rose upon the sea,

the black clouds moved through the stars, and a little boat came to take Fidella to the ship. Once aboard, the maiden was given a pretty cottage with a garden to be her very own.

And, sailing by night and by day, furrowing vast and lonely seas, the giant ship came to the wood beyond the world.

The fountain of memory lay at the foot of the noblest of the trees, and the silvery music of its falling water was the only sound to be heard in all the wood. A hooded figure of worn and ancient stone, standing with head bowed low, held aloft the jar from which it flowed, an endless crystal stream.

And Fidella, stooping to fill her cup in the basin of stone below, saw mirrored in the water there, gathering and dissolving one into the other, memories of all the years of her life which had been.

Once more through the lonely seas sailed the giant ship of Airda the Queen, Fidella again beheld the land, and presently she fared over hill and dale to the Kingdom of the Fields.

The winter was over and gone, and all the towns and villages of the realm were decked with bannerets and wreaths of early flowers, for in three days' time the Lord Alois was to wed the Princess Melusine.

Presently Fidella, journeying through the land, arrived on the crest of a hill overlooking the royal city and, pausing there a while, took counsel with herself as to how she might best make her way to Alois and offer him the cup of memory.

"I must find me a loom," said faithful Fidella, "and weave upon it a wedding gift so worthy that the lords of the castle will suffer me to go with it to Alois."

And she sought out a house and a loom in a village by the city, and paid for them with a penny of gold. And from one neighbor she had silver yarn; and from another, blue; and from others, all the colors of the world.

Fidella knelt at the edge of the pool, and filled her golden cup with the waters of memory

And now Fidella began to weave a fair tapestry picture of the story she had lived, beginning the tale with the golden light in the wood and the coming of Alois to the glade. Thread by thread, inch by inch, the grass-palace of Airda grew on the loom, the cave of the talking waters, the giant ship with its masts above the clouds, and the fountain of memory in the wood beyond the world. The sun set behind the high towers of the city, and still Fidella labored at the loom; candles melted low, and still the sound of the weaving hummed upon the air.

In the dark of the second night, as Fidella rose to toss a brand upon the fire, she heard, through the quiet of the room, the distant beat of galloping hoofs and the thundering rumble of a coach. Louder and louder grew the sound, and presently there passed the maiden's dwelling a huge coach speeding from the city. Strange to tell, its lanterns were unlit and its curtains closely drawn.

"Perchance some noble guest hath been

summoned posthaste to his realm," thought Fidella.

And now it was the morn, the marriage morn of the Knight Alois and the Princess Melusine. Alas, still unfinished was the picture tapestry! Fearing to risk a single moment more, however, the maiden unbound the picture from the loom and, carrying the gift and her golden cup, joined the merrymakers thronging to the city. The streets were already full of soldiers in gayest uniforms, strolling musicians, young nobles, larking pages, good countryfolk, and sober burgesses in velvet gowns. Those who brought gifts for Alois and Melusine were faring into the castle through the eastern gate.

The bells of the castle were ringing as they never rang before.

Fidella approached to the portal with her gift. A haughty chamberlain, with a silver chain about his shoulders, stood there by the thresh-hold and suffered only those to enter in whom he thought well worthy of the boon.

"But my good young woman," said the chamberlain severely to Fidella, "your tapestry is unfinished still. Go to your home and weave it to an end ere you return again. You may not enter."

"Oh, sir," cried poor Fidella, "do not thrust me back! Let me enter, I pray; oh, let me go within!"

"What I have said, I have said," replied the chamberlain, shouting at Fidella through the deafening clangor of the bells. "Young woman, I forbid — "

Suddenly the bells stopped in the middle of a peal, and everything grew very strangely still. People began to look questioningly at one another.

The Princess Melusine was not to be found! She had fled during the night with her cousin, the King of the Golden Hill. The coach, which Fidella had seen, had borne the runaway bride. As for the knight Alois, some said that he had already left the realm, whilst others murmured that he was hiding for shame in a tower. And many laughed.

Thrust from the portal by the guards, Fidella returned to her cottage in the fields.

And now it was night, the air was sweet with the fragrance of earth beneath the plough, and a sickle moon hung in the cloudy west with the old moon in her arms. Within her silent house Fidella kindled a yellow fire, threw the tapestry picture over the loom, and stood by the hearth gazing deep into the flame.

Suddenly a knocking sounded at the door, and Fidella, answering the summons, found herself standing face to face with the young knight, Alois. His pride touched to the quick, the forsaken youth had lingered in the castle till the dark, and then fled with his people from the town. And, because he had fled in haste and was athirst, the youth had paused at the first light shining in the fields.

Standing on the threshold in the moonlight, the youth asked a cup of water of the maid.

With a beating heart, Fidella lifted to his hands the cup of memory.

And now there came an end to the enchanter's wicked spell and the long years of danger and faithful questing. Letting fall the golden cup, the young knight uttered a great cry and stretched out his arms to the faithful maid for whose sake he had braved the anger of the King, the loyal maid who had loved him with a loving faith and braved many a peril for him through the kingdoms of the world.

"Dear Fidella," said Alois, "to-day is the day of my coming-of-age, and I am free forever of the King. Now shall you be the Lady of my land. Come; my people and my coach are at the door."

So now Fidella quenched the taper, leaving only a flickering brand to light the empty room, and walked with Alois to the coach. A little breeze was stirring in the grass, and somewhere in a glen beyond the fields a bird awoke, sang a few sweet piping notes, and then was still.

"I am glad I did not finish my tapestry," whispered Fidella; "for now I can weave it to a merry close."

And the coach rolled away, over hill, over dale, in the golden light of the moon.

THE PARSON CAPEN HOUSE
TOPSFIELD, MASSACHUSETTS